Who Murdered Mary Christmas?

A Josephine Stuart Mystery

by

Joyce Oroz

This book is fiction. All characters, events, and organizations portrayed in this novel are the product of the author's imagination or are used fictitiously. Any resemblance to actual persons—living or dead—is entirely coincidental.

For information, email **Cozy Cat Press**,
cozycatpress@aol.com or visit our website at:
www.cozycatpress.com

COZY CAT
PRESS

ISBN: 978-1-946063-01-4

Printed in the United States of America

Cover design by Paula Ellenberger
www.paulaellenberger.com

1 2 3 4 5 6 7 8 9 10

I would like to thank a special person in my life who has helped me with this book and all my other books. My husband, Art Oroz, is a walking dictionary. He helps me whenever spell-check fails. He sees the finished manuscript before anyone else, reads it and tells me what makes sense and what doesn't, sometimes offering solutions for the unbelievable situations I come up with.

A big thank you goes to Avery, Laura and Jeff for their technical help.

I also want to thank Marlene and Tomi for their continuing support and encouragement of my series of stories.

I also want to thank the wonderful folks at Cozy Cat Press for their part in bringing this book to the public.

Chapter 1

One blustery November afternoon, six adult art students, under the able direction of Ms. Kati, shivered on cold benches balancing watercolor papers taped to breadboards on our laps. A blinding silver sun hovered over the choppy Pacific Ocean. Suddenly a gust of wind ripped my wet watercolor painting from its board. Strands of auburn hair slapped my face giving my eyes a moment of relief from the sun. When I pushed the hair back I saw my painting lying on damp grass, face down, a couple feet away. I lunged for it but the wind got there first and whipped the paper into the air.

Over the roar of pounding waves a seagull screamed.

Scrambling after the painting, I ran to my left across the grass, made a sharp right turn toward the sun and slip-slided down a short bank to a walking trail below. When my feet finally hit the blacktopped surface, I barely missed stepping on a little white cattle dog trotting along, its leash dragging. A bicycle rider wearing black sweat pants and jacket, ooga, oogad a rusty horn impatiently as the bike rolled by.

Shading my eyes with one hand, I searched the empty path. There was no sign of a painting, so I thought I would check in on Mary Milford and ask for her help. Contrary Mary was a fellow student in Kati's watercolor class. I hoped she'd noticed where my picture had landed. Ms. Mary, true to form, had broken from the group of students and used the lower walking trail as her vantage-point. Her paint box and half-finished painting rested on a bench, but she was not around.

I walked about a hundred yards down the path, but there was not a living soul on or near the trail so I headed back to Mary's bench, admitting to myself that my watercolor image of a choppy ocean at high tide had probably landed in the waves and was being salt-watered to death.

Checking out my theory, I crossed the path and glanced fifty feet down at angry winter waves attacking giant rocks at the base of the cliff.

"Darn it! All that work and it's ruined," I groaned out loud to the wind, as incessant waves slapped what looked like my picture around like a flag in a hurricane.

My head snapped back for a second look at what I hoped I hadn't seen—a red hand-knitted sweater with pearl buttons swirling in the foamy water, the red sweater Mary wore as she worked on her last painting in front of her last sunset. It was the sweater that had caught in the door earlier in the day when half a dozen students piled into Kati's van, anticipating an inspiring session of plein-air painting.

I had signed up for the watercolor class because my friend Alicia had suggested we try it out. Besides, we had already paid for a table and wall-space at the upcoming Holiday Art Festival held at the Aromas Grange where we hoped to sell a few paintings.

Since watercolor techniques are opposite acrylic and oil methods of painting, it took several classes with Kati before I was able to produce a half-decent painting. Watercolor requires planning, a light touch, and light colors first, darker ones last and every stroke executed correctly the first time around—a tough concept to grasp for an impatient fifty-year-old muralist.

Once Alicia and I had attended multiple evening classes held at a Watsonville elementary school, practicing the basic watercolor principles *ad nauseam*, we were finally able to advance to Kati's outdoor class just in time for winter's worst. Our teacher watched the weather channel religiously, hoping to outwit El Nino and the incoming winter storms.

Three days went by before rescuers found a body and two more days passed before we knew for sure it was Mary who had drowned in the ocean.

Saturday evening, November 30th, exactly seven days after the accident, our class met once again in the Watsonville classroom due to bad weather.

Kati called for a moment of silence for our departed classmate.

Mr. Buzznick looked uncomfortable sitting on a tiny wooden chair, his knees trapped under a fourth-grader's desk. He adjusted his eye-patch as his lower lip quivered. A tear escaped from his good eye, not surprising since anybody could see that he had been hitting on poor old Mary regularly. Apparently, she had wanted a guy with two good eyes, or maybe she had been playing hard-to-get.

Plucky Claudia Batson obviously thought Buzz was a real catch. But Claudia's eyes weren't exactly 20-20. Her glasses were so thick and heavy that they slipped down her nose to rest on the knob at the end. Every minute or so she would wrinkle her nose, forcing the glasses upward, only to have them slide south all over again.

Another student, Vick Smathers had his eyes on my best friend, Alicia, even though she was half his age and married, and he was old as dirt. Vick wore his dyed black hair slicked back with something greasy. He smelled like tobacco and mothballs and he wore an "Elvis Lives" button on his stained sweater vest. But the man could paint. Vick had a steady hand and real talent in the watercolor department.

My friend Alicia also had talent. Her watercolor paintings ranked close to Kati's, up there in the "fantastic range." I wasn't surprised at her ability because we'd been working together for years, painting murals all over Santa Cruz and Monterey Counties. As a seventeen-year-long widow, it was what I did for a living, and what kept Alicia in pocket money. Her husband Ernie Quintana, biology professor at UCSC, supported Alicia and their ten-year-old son, Trigger, very well.

The only student not in attendance was Marla, Mary's younger sister—at least she looked and acted younger. Marla was a bit taller, straighter and slimmer than her sister, and her naturally red hair hadn't gone completely grey, but her hands always shook, giving her paintings a "Van Gogh look."

Kati taped a piece of twelve by sixteen inch cold-pressed Strathmore rag-paper onto a slightly larger board. Buzz, Claudia, Vick, Alicia and I followed suit, attaching heavy paper to our boards. The room was uncomfortably quiet. Nothing spilled, dropped or broke. No one split a fingernail or twisted an ankle. Not even a sneeze. Mary had been our maker of noise, our disrupter, giggler and most awkward classmate-princess. It was easy to imagine the plump little lady all wibbly-wobbly, poking along the cliffs, oblivious to the wind until it jerked her around and blew her away.

The void Mary left behind was quiet and sad.

Without warning, the windowed door to the fourth grade classroom opened and two sheriff's deputies entered, folded their arms and waited to be announced.

"Class, I forgot to tell you…ah, these officers want to ask you some questions about last Saturday," Kati said. "They think Mary was murdered."

We all sucked in some air at the same moment. Jaws dropped and eyes bugged as the thought of murder sunk in.

"This is Officer Lund." Kati pointed to a tall slender woman with blond hair pulled into a tight bun and ice-blue eyes that squinted when they met mine.

"And this is Officer Sayer." Kati pointed to a shorter, thicker, darker person, his frizzy hair going grey, his warm brown eyes relaxed. His full lips smiled when he saw me. I had run into this team before.

"I'll start with you, Ms. Stuart," Officer Sayer said. "Did you see anyone on the lower walking trail last Saturday?"

I shook my head and answered, "No, except for a dog and a bicyclist. In fact, I was looking for Mary because my painting flew away and I thought she might have seen where it landed. Actually, my painting landed in the water just a couple feet from Mary's red sweater."

"Thank you, Josephine. I know this is difficult for you—for all of you who knew the deceased," Officer Sayer addressed the cluster of stunned students looking up from their miniature chairs and desks.

I raised my hand, feeling like a fourth-grader needing to go to the lavatory.

"Officer Sayer, I have a question. What makes you think Mary was murdered?"

Officer Lund pursed her thin lips and answered for Sayer. She said it was an on-going investigation and they could not tell us why murder was being considered. And then she asked me to describe the bicyclist.

I thought for a moment. "I couldn't see the face very well between the knitted hat pulled low and a scarf wrapped over the mouth. I remember skinny black sweat pants and I think there was a backpack…blue, I think. Dark blue."

"Thank you, Josephine."

Lund jotted something into her notebook and pointed to Buzz.

"Sir, did you see Mary or anyone else on the lower trail?"

"Yeah, I saw Mary…checked on her every so often. She was too close to the cliff for bein' awkward like she was, poor thing. My watch-timer went off at four o'clock, so I went back to the van to take my pills. When guys get to a certain age they gotta take pills…anyway, when I got back to my painting, the wind was blowin' hard. I decided to go down the trail and check on Mary. That's when I found Josephine heading back with the bad news." He blinked his eye several times and wiped away a tear.

"Thank you, sir. You, the lady in the green dress, did you see anything?"

Claudia looked down to see what color dress she was wearing. "My name is Claudia Batson and I didn't see anything." Someone chuckled. "I didn't dare hike down to the lower trail because I had sprained my ankle a few days before, you see."

Vick stood up. "I went down to check out the walking trail and stretch my legs around two-thirty. I checked out Mary's painting—not bad, but after that, I really got into my painting and all of a sudden it's after four and Josephine's hurrying across the parking lot lookin' all shook up." He sat down.

Officer Lund handed a card to each of us and Officer Sayer asked us to call if we thought of anything new, any detail that might help with the investigation. The officers slipped out the door and we went back to thinking and painting in silence. I tried not to think about Mary's unexpected demise, but watching the officers leave the room triggered a memory from last Saturday. I remembered sliding down the bank to the trail, steadying myself with one hand and shielding my eyes with the other. A person paragliding about twenty feet from the cliff caught my attention. The parachute-looking contraption eclipsed the sun for a moment, and in that moment of relief for my eyes, I remembered thinking how bright that must be for the person flying west toward the sun. Even as I watched, the wind suddenly bounced the glider into a right turn, pushing him north toward the cove.

"Earth to Josephine, earth to Josephine…" Alicia whispered.

"What's going on?" I asked, looking across the room at a cluster of students.

As Kati demonstrated another sky technique, Alicia and I crowded around to see how it was done. Our teacher quickly painted a deep phthalo blue sky onto damp paper. As soon as the paint covered the upper half of the paper, Kati put down her one-inch brush and sprinkled a handful of salt over the wet paint, instantly creating stars. A moment later, using a cotton swab, she carefully lifted wet paint off the paper leaving behind the shape of a crescent moon. Everyone sighed and went back to their seats to try their luck—or skill as the case might be.

"Jo, do you remember the skateboarders zooming down the trail last Saturday?"

"Yeah, I saw three of them. But that was around noon. Do you think one of them came back later and accidentally ran into Mary?"

"Well, the police seem to think she didn't fall on her own," Alicia said as she swished dark blue pigment over her damp paper.

"We need to find out why the police think it was murder. That would be a place to start." I wiped the paper with a wet brush.

"Sorry I brought it up. Now you want to solve the mystery, right?"

"I'm as curious as anyone…." I painted in a dark blue sky.

"You're ten times more curious than anyone I know," she laughed. "Wait till David finds out you have another murder mystery to solve." She sprinkled salt on the wet paint and watched stars appear.

"David is becoming more comfortable with my hobby."

"Some hobby." Alicia rolled her eyes. She leaned over her picture and blew the salt away.

"I can't help it if I was the one who discovered the sweater when Mary rolled into the ocean." I sprinkled salt on my sky. Unfortunately the stars didn't come out because the paint had already dried. Being anxious—maybe over anxious—to create six or eight really nice pictures to sell at the annual Art Festival didn't help. Alicia and I had attended the event every year for years and talked about selling our artwork there someday. In October we went so far as to pay for a table space. Now the pressure was on to create and frame as many watercolor masterpieces as possible before December 21st. It was already the end of November. We had three weeks to put a show together.

Was that a hot flash I felt—or fear of failure?

"Jo, you're turning red."

"Wait till you're a half century old and see if you don't turn red." Perspiration ran down my forehead.

"I know you, Jo. Don't sweat the small stuff. We'll get our act together in time for the show."

"At least you will. Your painting is looking good."

"This is our next-to-last class before the festival, so let's get together tomorrow and paint like crazy, okay?" she said, enthusiastically.

I nodded, rolled up my failed painting and packed up my paint box. We pulled on our hooded jackets and ran across the schoolyard to the parking lot where my red Mazda pickup was parked. I popped the snug-top up, deposited our paint equipment in the bed of the truck and closed the lid before the rain could spoil Alicia's artwork. Shivering in the dimly lit parking lot, we hurriedly climbed into our seats; I turned the key and jacked up the heater and the wipers.

Five minutes later, we cruised through Alicia's neighborhood where her two-story house stood at the edge of Drew Lake. The lights were on, the boys were home. The rain had lightened up.

"Good night, Allie."

"Night, Jo." She gathered her art equipment from the back of my truck and disappeared into the house.

I turned the truck around and headed for the Aromas hills and my little adobe house on five grassy acres of oak trees, blue jays, poison oak and miles of gopher tunnels. I imagined myself painting like mad for the next couple weeks, but had no clue what the subject matter would be. My last mural job had ended two days ago and the next one wouldn't start until January. The nice part about murals was that most clients already knew what they wanted me to paint.

Ten miles and fifteen minutes passed quickly due to deep thoughts about deadlines and murder. But once I reached home, Solow's wagging tail quickly brought me back to rational thinking and the care taking of my faithful companion. I poured kibble and fresh water for my basset buddy and a good helping of ice cream for me and my nerves. My imagination was bigger than my appetite, so a portion of ice cream went to Solow.

I picked up my cell phone and played back a message from my next door neighbor, David Galaz, just to hear his voice. He told me he'd be staying in Modesto with his son and granddaughter for a couple days. A few days apart would make our together times all the sweeter.

Smiling in the dark, I listened to Solow's snores across the room, and wondered what David was doing at that very moment. Did he miss me the way I missed him?

Chapter 2

Morning was a relief after a series of tumultuous dreams and nightmares. I woke up breathless from falling into the cold Pacific Ocean, being dragged under the water, smashed against jagged rocks, then climbing the steep cliff wearing a red sweater, and carrying a slippery salmon under my arm, only to be pushed back into the water by the hand of a faceless being. I must have been whimpering in my sleep because I opened my eyes to Solow's worried gaze and a lick across my cheek. I pushed the nightmare out of my head and sat up.

"Okay, time to get up. Need to go outside?"

Solow woofed as I pulled on my robe. We lumbered down the hall to the back door. I opened it and immediately he was off, running after David's cat, Fluffy, better known as, "Miss Two-face." She was a sweet lovable girl until it came to teasing my poor dog. That's when she would morph into a vexatious tormentor. Over the years she had led Solow on many a futile chase, sometimes through tall grass and poison oak, sometimes under fences and down into gullies, but in the end it was always the same. Fluffy won the race and my short-legged boy would crawl home, tail tucked between his legs.

I put on the coffee and dropped a bagel in the toaster, subconsciously listening for a bark from Solow wanting to come back in. I had made up my mind not to read the newspaper or make phone calls. My new schedule would consist of watercolor painting and nothing else.

Since Solow was obviously enjoying the outdoors, I ate my breakfast, cleaned the kitchen, showered and dressed and periodically peeked out the window to see if he'd come home. But he hadn't. What was taking so long?

I taped a sheet of watercolor paper to a board and set my brushes, pallet and tubes of paint on the dining room table. The light was good there. I filled a jug of water and thumbed through pictures cut out of magazines, saved for this very purpose. Three scenes inspired me, somewhat. But Solow wasn't back. He hadn't had his breakfast. I couldn't concentrate on painting until he came home.

For the fiftieth time I glanced out the window, but this time a large white cat stared back at me from the top of a fence post about ten yards from where I stood in the dining room. Fluffy wasn't preening herself. She just stared directly into my window.

I hurried outside and down the uneven brick path, took a turn into the cold wet weeds and walked straight to Fluffy's post. She leaped down, swished her tail and disappeared under the wild lilac bushes lining a four-foot deep drainage ditch that stretched the length of my property. The ditch paralleled Otis Road as it ran under my driveway through a large concrete pipe. I listened to the watery echo emanating from the pipe, hoping to hear Solow.

An unusual amount of water had accumulated from recent rains.

Cold droplets of water showered my head and shoulders as I stood under wet lilac bushes trying to decide what to do next. Where was that rascally cat?

I called out to Solow. No answer. I crept further along the ditch, following the flow of rain water as it headed toward David's property. Hunched over, I sloshed through a concrete pipe under his driveway where two-foot-deep muddy water rushed toward lower ground. My Levis were soaked up to my knees and my feet felt like popsicles.

Suddenly Fluffy reappeared at the side of the ditch looking dry and beautiful as ever. She stopped in front of a snag of debris caught in the frothy water at the far corner of David's property.

I thought I heard something. "Solow…Solow, where are you?"

"Woof…woof," was followed by a long mournful howl that tore my heart to pieces.

I charged into the debris, tossing rusted metal and warped wood aside until I saw my buddy tangled in a mass of plastic refuse. Holding everything together was a scramble of fishing line. I debated whether I should run home for scissors, but as I considered the pros and cons, Solow whined. He looked cold and scared. I couldn't leave him, so I frantically raked the pile with my bare hands until a space opened up, allowing Solow to push his way out of the mess.

We sloshed along in the ditch until we found a narrow deer trail leading up to David's side yard, and stopped to rest on his patio furniture. Fluffy sat on my boyfriend's new barbeque, grooming her long white fluff with a practiced tongue while I seethed ten feet away on a cold wet bench. Solow was exhausted, but he held no grudges. When he'd finally licked himself dry, we set out across David's back yard and then across mine.

The kitchen phone rang as we walked in the back door. I felt a small surge of energy and sprang for it.

"Hello?"

"Jo, you sound winded. I'm having trouble concentrating," Alicia said. "How are you doing?"

"Not so good. Maybe if you come over we can inspire each other."

"I was thinking the same thing—be right over."

I changed into a dry pair of Levis, t-shirt, socks and shoes, and then worried about what I'd make for lunch. In that moment I realized why I loved mural painting. No interruptions, no housework, no problems, just drive to work and paint.

Solow watched with fascination as I ripped apart and chopped up the meat from a leftover chicken carcass. Doggie drool puddled on the floor as he leaned into my calf, letting me know how much he loved and adored my chicken. But he lost focus when I brought out the lettuce, apple and arugula. He sauntered into the living room to lay by the fire, missing the last step—my homemade honey-mustard dressing.

If only I could relax like Solow. Monday's yoga class might do the trick. I didn't go often because I was usually working, but whenever I did go, it was quite a wonderful workout.

Alicia pounded on the front door.

I opened it. "Allie, want to go to yoga tomorrow with me?"

"Ah, I guess so…but don't we need to paint?" She placed her paint box next to mine on the dining room table and followed me into the kitchen.

"We'll be home by noon. We'll have hours and hours to paint," I said, as I shoved the bowl of chicken salad into the fridge. A couple things in the back fell over—I made a mental note to clean it up later.

For the next half hour, I sorted through Alicia's magazine pictures hoping to be inspired, and she looked through mine. We drank cups of tea. Time ticked by. We ate chicken salad for lunch. The clock ticked away. Finally, we came up with a plan. Alicia picked a picture for me to paint and I picked one for her.

"Papers are taped securely to the boards, start your engines," I said, shaking my little bottle of frisket, a square of kneaded rubber at the ready. I taped my assigned magazine picture, a quaint farmhouse surrounded on three sides by green grass and a few cherry trees, to the dining room wall. Alicia taped her assigned picture, a lazy green river with three colorful row boats upside down on the beach, next to mine.

I used a pencil to sketch the farmhouse while Alicia penciled in a horizon line, the curve of the river and three boats. We opened our bottles of frisket and dabbed the milky goo with Q-tips wherever we needed highlights. I dabbed it liberally on the blooming cherry trees and one angle of the farmhouse roof.

Once the dabbing was done, we started on the sky, always moving from top to bottom, background to foreground. We quickly wet the sky area with water. I slathered Cobalt Blue across the top of the paper, wet my brush and pulled ziggy trails of blue down toward the horizon, and then swirled a faint yellow into the lower atmosphere. I mixed a tiny bit of cobalt blue into some hookers green and painted in the far away hills.

I let Solow outside for a run and went back to painting.

The phone rang. I let it ring.

Alicia and I were making real progress. Magenta mingled with ultramarine blue in Alicia's summer sky. I added blue, grey and violet to the mountains ringing the valley where the frisketed farmhouse soaked up the sun. Green grass and wildflowers covered the sloping foreground.

"Jo, did you hear that?"

"I'm trying to concentrate here, but yes, I heard it. Sounded like brakes." We put down our brushes and hurried to the front door. I opened it and gasped.

"Solow…Solow sweetie…are you all right?" I ran to his side.

Solow cried.

"Sorry, ma'am," the clean-cut man wearing a brown shirt and shorts uniform in December said. "Didn't see him till it was too late. He was chasing this really big white cat…."

"It's not your fault," I moaned as I knelt down to examine my shivering dog standing on three paws. I petted him and touched him everywhere. When I got to his right hind paw, he cried. The foot didn't look right and it was swelling even as I squatted on the ground trying to comfort him.

The UPS delivery driver offered to carry Solow into the house, but I asked him to put my dog in the passenger seat of my pickup instead. Alicia and I watched as Solow yelped, and then became quiet. I cracked the passenger window open and closed the door.

"Jo, I know you want to take care of Solow right now. I'm sure he'll be okay." She gave me a hug and said, "I'll take my painting home and finish it there. At least we got a good start."

"We did pretty well…I'm going to take Solow directly to the doc. See you at yoga tomorrow," I said as we dashed into the house.

Alicia gathered up her painting and paint box and headed out to her green Volvo.

I grabbed my purse and darted out the door.

Mr. UPS handed over a package, as he uttered ten huge apologies, hurried back to his truck and started the engine.

I followed the boxy brown truck down Otis with Alicia's car right behind me. I thought about turning back and locking the front door since Solow would not be home to protect the house, but on the other hand, I wanted to get him to the doctor as soon as possible. We flew down San Juan Road to Watsonville. The sun hung low in the sky, like the day Mary had lost her life. I wondered for the hundredth time, how the police knew she was murdered. And why would someone murder a nice middle-aged lady like Mary? I needed to talk to her sister, Marla, who coincidentally had been going to my yoga class for years but neither of us was exactly regular with our attendance. We were both busy women and we went when we had time.

Solow raised his head and looked around the parking lot. I found an empty space at the rear of Dr. Finley's office and slipped my pickup neatly into it. As I carried Solow into the building, I felt his heart beating double-time. Finley was good with animals, but Solow had an excellent memory when it came to previous doctor visits that included shots and medicines.

Stopping at the reception desk, I explained my emergency. I was told to sit and wait. Solow's long body kept slipping off my lap. Finally, I placed him on the floor. He stood on three legs. I leaned down to pet his long velvety ears.

"Quite a dog ya got there, Josephine," a man's voice rumbled across the room.

I looked up. "Oh, Buzz, what are you doing here?" Then I saw a cage full of scrawny yellow cat on the floor beside his chair. "I hope nothing's wrong with your cat."

"Everything's wrong with him. He's not going home this time."

I thought about that, not going home? Where would he go? Oh, no. He was about to go to kitty heaven. A tear escaped from under Buzz's eye patch and ran down his cheek. He sniffed and squirmed in his chair.

The lady at the desk called, "Mr. Buzznick."

He picked up the cage and bravely carried it into the inner sanctum of veterinary medicine featuring shortcuts to heaven.

I flipped through a magazine to take my mind off the poor kitty. A full-page color picture of a tropical sunset caught my eye. It had everything—ocean, beach, palm trees and a fabulous sunset. The receptionist was on the phone—head down—writing. I quickly, quietly worked the tropical scene loose from the magazine.

The receptionist looked up.

My cheeks heated up as I stuffed the folded paper into my purse.

"Ms. Stuart," she said, "the doctor will see you now. Do you need help lifting Solow?"

I nodded. I hadn't thought to bring Solow's leash. He would rather run away on four broken paws than voluntarily walk into one of Dr. Finley's examination rooms.

A muscular male nurse appeared from the inner sanctum, gently picked up Solow and headed down the hall toward our assigned room. I gathered my coat and purse and hurried to catch up to my buddy. As I walked past the front desk, the receptionist pointed to a stack of magazines on the floor in the corner behind her desk and asked if I'd like to take them home.

I told the woman, "Yes, I'd love to have them. Thank you."

By the time I got to Solow's room, the nurse had him resting on the stainless steal table in the center of the room. The nurse stepped out of the room and I took his place, petting Solow and making sure he stayed on the table.

Half an hour later, Dr. Finley let himself into the little room and offered Solow a treat. My sweet dog resisted as long as he could, knowing from past experience that it was a bribe. Finally, he gave in and gulped the little nugget.

"Is it just the paw?" Dr. Finley asked.

"As far as I know."

He pushed and prodded Solow all over but only found a sore foot. After taking an x-ray, Finley said that two digits had hairline fractures. He left the room. The nurse arrived, handed me a bottle of pain killers and quickly fitted Solow with a Velcro boot. Solow followed me to the door on three legs, happy to be leaving.

"Ms. Stuart, that will be $358."

Solow stood at my side. "Can you take credit?" I asked, feeling faint from sticker-shock.

"Certainly, and don't forget your magazines." She ran my card, I signed. I lifted the box of magazines and carried them across the modestly lit parking lot. Solow hobbled along at my side. As soon as the magazines were deposited into the back of the truck, he whimpered for me to give him a hike into the front seat where he proceeded to curl up and fall asleep.

Preparing to back out of the parking space, I noticed the vehicle next to mine, a classic white Mustang with blue racing stripes. A man sat in the driver's seat, his bald head resting on the steering wheel.

I cut the engine, climbed out of the cab and walked to the man's half-open window.

"Hey, Buzz, are you okay?"

Buzz cranked his head around and looked up with his left eye.

"Josephine…I, ah…you know…sniff." He rolled the window all the way down.

"We sure love our pets," I said, for lack of anything better to say. "My dog just cost me $358."

"Murphy only cost a hundred, but I don't get to take him ho—ome." Sniff.

Wanting to redirect Buzz's train of thought, I asked, "Have you heard any more about Mary's fall, like why they think it was murder?"

"Well, her boyfriend might know something," he growled.

"Oh," I said, watching his face twist at the thought of the boyfriend. "Guess I better get Solow home. See you at the Art Festival…you're going aren't you?"

"Oh, sure, I'll be selling my hand carved wine stoppers and a few birdhouses. I'm sure you gals will have the watercolor market cornered."

"Wish I was sure of that. Take it easy, Buzz." I waved goodbye. Solow was fast asleep when I climbed in beside him. I rearranged his sprawling back leg—the good one, pushing it onto the seat. His long body never did fit the seat very well. His usual posture was, tail wagging, head out the window and ears flying like whirligigs. But at that moment, he looked like a precious child—adorable, sleeping, and unaware of traffic and bad weather.

Solow woke up when I pulled to a stop in front of the house. He followed me inside on three legs. A flash of white fur ran out the door as we entered. Poor Fluffy must have been locked in the house alone. Then I saw it—my painting on the dining room table. The closer I got, the worse it looked. Dirty paw prints were everywhere. I touched the paper. It felt warm.

"You stupid cat! You slept on my painting!" I pounded the table with my fist.

Solow slinked into the living room.

"Not you, Solow; I'm not mad at you…." I ran after him to reassure him that I was not a crazy tyrant.

Chapter 3

Monday morning was spent stretching and posing in Sonia's yoga class with Alicia and about fifteen other women. The class was open to men but the few who tried it never lasted long. Sonia had actually forgotten my name it had been so long since I'd attended. Working Monday through Friday meant yoga only happened between mural jobs. Actually, my painting work typically involved a lot of reaching, stretching and balancing. When I wasn't painting murals I was usually reticent to drive the fifteen minutes to class and back.

"Are you feeling calmer, Jo?" Alicia asked at the end of class.

"Yeah, calm enough to take a nap," I croaked. "Maybe a cup of tea would help."

We gathered our jackets, purses and weights—if you call two pounders weights, and left the hospital's library-multi-purpose room. Outside, the sun seemed extra bright in the crisp clean air. Christmas decorations were already up and Watsonville was looking festive. I drove us to a local coffee shop where we sat in a booth by the window and ordered cups of tea.

"I can't wait to get started on my next painting," Alicia said over the roar of a flappochinasita machine. "I'm going to paint from a calendar picture of a Mexican village."

"Yeah, I think I'll paint a picture of Fluffy today," I grinned. "I wonder how she'd look all tied up on a spit over a campfire, her white hair turning brown like an over cooked marshmallow, kind of a western campfire scene."

Alicia rolled her eyes.

I wondered if she had ever had an evil thought in her life, probably not.

The front door of the café opened and a middle-aged woman walked up to our table.

"Marla," I stuttered. "We missed you at painting class and I looked for you at yoga today."

"And Marla," Alicia said, "we're so sorry about your sister. Mary was a lovely lady." My friend stood up and hugged the woman wearing blue everything. Her eyes were rimmed in red.

"How have you been, Marla?" I asked, following Alicia's example of kindness and caring.

"I try to be cheerful, but it's tough...." she sniffed. "I hear you two are going to be in the art show at the grange this year. Are you excited?"

"Unprepared," I crabbed.

"Jo's having cat-trouble," Alicia explained. "The neighbor's cat ruined her last painting."

Marla checked her watch. "I'm picking up donuts for my book club. We meet in twenty minutes. See you later." She headed for the back of the line at the counter.

"Excuse me, Allie, I need to ask Marla something." I stood at the end of the line behind Mary's sister.

"Excuse me, Marla, did you ever find out why the sheriffs think it was murder?" I whispered.

She whipped her head around. "No one told me it was murder...."

Everyone in the coffee shop turned to look at Marla.

"You haven't talked to the deputies?"

"No, when did you talk to them?"

"At the last painting class...."

"Oh, well they must be wrong. Who would want to kill Mary?" She moved forward to the counter. I went back to my seat by the window and watched Marla purchase her sack of donuts. She carried it out the door and climbed into a white SUV with Claudia sitting in the passenger seat. As Marla quickly cut into the flow of traffic, I wondered who else belonged to the book club, then gave myself a mental slap on the head for being nosey.

"Finish your tea, Jo. We have work to do," Alicia said with a smile.

"You're right, but I'm almost afraid to try again."

I dropped Alicia at her home on my way to the grocery store. The store was practically empty at eleven o'clock in the morning. My favorite employee, a young man named Robert, saw me coming and pushed an empty shopping cart my way. The string on his apron hung below his belly, freckles sprinkled his face and his smile revealed braces across his front teeth. As young as he was, he knew a lot for his age—always keeping up with the news, always interesting to talk to.

"Hey, Josephine, heard about the murder on the Capitola cliffs?"

"Are you talking about Mary Milford?"

"Yeah, I heard the area's taped off like a crime scene," Robert said.

"Actually, I was there that day and I was the one who saw her sweater in the water." The memory sent an uncomfortable chill through my body.

"Hey, Jo, are you all right?" Robert asked.

"I think so. What else have you heard about the murder?"

"Well, my mom walks on that trail all the time and she said she remembers seeing a lady wearing a red sweater sitting on a bench painting and talking to a little girl. Mom said she remembers because the girl was speaking Spanish and so was the woman."

"I didn't know Mary spoke Spanish…." I said, as Robert held up a good-sized pineapple.

"Got some really good pineapples over here." He pointed to a neat stack of them. "Unless you want pears or apples?"

A light bulb blinked on in my head.

"I'll take three apples, a pineapple and two pears." I bagged the fruit, feeling excited about my new plan. I would paint a still life from a lovely pile of fruit. Driving home I thought about how the picture would look, and what the background and lighting should be. I hurried into the house, set the bag of fruit on the kitchen counter and bent down to give my gimpy dog some love.

With lunch, dishes, a trip to David's to check on Fluffy's food and more lovin' for Solow out of the way, I arranged, rearranged and arranged again the fruit on a blue ceramic platter. Finally, it suited me, but before I began painting I threw a load of clothes in the washing machine, and let Solow out the back door. Together we walked to the end of the driveway and collected the mail from the mailbox. Solow made the trip on three legs with no complaints.

Back in the house, I jumped into my painting project by taping watercolor paper to a board and penciling in the fruit. Next came the frisketed areas, future highlights. I painted a lavender background, ignoring the real background consisting of windows and drapes in my dining room, reassuring myself that artists do this all the time. It was called "artistic license." As my eighth grade art teacher used to say, "If I wanted an exact picture of something I'd have taken a photograph of it."

The phone rang.

"Hello."

"Hi, Josie. You sound a little up-tight. What's wrong, honey?"

"Hi, David, I'm supposed to be painting but I just can't concentrate...."

"Are you sure you're all right...?"

"It's nothing really. I just need to get a few paintings finished. Only three weeks left...."

"You can do it, Josie; I know you can. You've wanted to do this for years. You can do it. Take a deep breath and start painting. I'm coming home Wednesday."

"Thank you, David, for the vote of confidence. See you Wednesday."

As we hung up, I thought about how convenient it was to have my boyfriend right next door and then I thought about Wednesday. How would I find time to paint and be with my guy? I wouldn't want to send the wrong message and hurt David's feelings. But time raced—the art show loomed.

Wishing to relax my mind, I thought about David's family—his son Harley and his five-year-old granddaughter Monica. Why hadn't he talked about them? Maybe I cut him off with my selfish worries. It wouldn't be the first time.

The phone rang. I groaned.

"Hello...oh hi, Mom, what's going on?"

"I just got home from the spa...I'm feeling so relaxed," she sighed.

"Yeah, I'm glad...ah, I gotta go...."

"Honey, what's wrong? Did I call at a bad time?"

"I'm sorry, Mom. I'm just so frustrated because life keeps getting in the way of painting. Allie and I are sharing a booth at the Aromas Art Festival in less than three weeks. We paid for the spot in October and finally

I'm between mural jobs, but I can't seem to produce even one decent painting."

"I'll let you go, sweetheart. Remember to enjoy your day." She hung up.

Enjoy my day? What did she mean by that? Didn't she understand what I just told her? She was starting to sound like Allie and David—all butterflies and roses.

The sky rumbled outside as clouds moved in from the north.

By three o'clock, my pineapple was looking pretty good so I started on the apples. In real life they were red but I made them green. The pears ended up with a hint of orange. I liked the idea of warm greens and yellows in the fruit against a cool lavender backdrop.

"Was that thunder?" I asked Solow.

He didn't open his eyes. Oh to be so relaxed.

I painted the blue plate and added Payne's gray mixed with purple for the shadows, while a thunder and lightening battle moved across the darkening sky stamping its heavy feet like an irate teenager.

Solow slept.

I found my kneaded rubber eraser and scrubbed off all the frisket, which left bare white paper—better known as highlights. I squinted at the picture of fruit, and then I held it up to the mirror in the bathroom. Not a masterpiece, but not bad. I finally had one painting finished. With a fresh white matt and a dark frame it would be a keeper.

David called, sounding hesitant, or maybe the connection was bad because of rain pounding against the windows.

"Hi, David, what's wrong?" I said as I carried my painting into the bedroom and laid it on the bed for safe keeping. I closed the door and walked back to the dining room.

"I didn't want to disturb you, but thought I should call…because I know you…you're probably wondering what happened to Mary Milford."

"Yeah, I'm curious about it. How do you know about Mary?" I said, trying not to sound too curious.

"Harley told me all about it. He has a friend in the Santa Cruz Sheriff's Department, and he said there were footprints at the edge of the cliff."

"Were they Mary's?"

"Yeah, they were hers alright…."

"But wouldn't you expect to have her footprints there?" I said.

"The prints show that she was facing the path—her back to the cliff."

"Sounds like she was posing for a picture, maybe someone took her picture like that?"

"Just thought you'd want to know. You sound better, Josie, everything going okay?"

"Yes, everything's fine. I don't know why I get so worked up over nothing. I finally finished a painting and I feel good about it. I hope I wasn't rude…don't take it personally…."

"I've known you for ten years, Josie. Besides, anyone can get a little depressed in this crazy weather. It's raining dogs, cats and termites in Modesto. That reminds me, my house will be tented for termites after Christmas. Know any place I can stay for a couple nights?"

My face flushed, but David didn't know that.

"If I knew you were comin' I'd a baked a cake…."

"There's plenty of time to bake one. Can't wait to see you, Josie."

He hung up.

Thunder cracked sharply overhead. I watched as lightening danced around until it found a telephone pole to zap, namely the pole on Otis in front of my house.

The transformer sparked as my house went dark. It was a little after five o'clock and winter darkness had already settled in. I bumped around from room to room until I found a candle. A bit more bumping and I had a box of matches. I lit the candle and fired up my freestanding wood-burning stove in the living room.

My cell phone rang.

"Oh, hi, Allie."

"Just checking to see if you're feeling any better."

"Oh, sure, I finished a painting and my mood is so much better. Did you paint today?"

"Actually, I finished two paintings—a harbor scene and a desert. It does feel good to have a few paintings ready to frame."

"I wouldn't know. I only have one."

"It's a start, Jo, now you can start another one."

"Candlelight isn't conducive to watercolor painting."

"Don't tell me your lights are out. That's too bad. I won't be painting tonight either. Trigger has a parent-teacher thing tonight. Talk to you soon."

I put the phone back in my purse, lit five more candles and fed Solow.

For the first time in a long time, I wasn't hungry.

The storm raged outside. I heard a crack and a smack from the back of the house. Imagining the worst, I lit two more candles and put another log on the fire for extra comfort. I remembered stormy nights when I was a little girl. Mom popped Jiffy-pop popcorn over the fire in the fireplace and Dad played the piano. I loved it when the lights went out.

I talked to Mom and Dad on my cell phone until it ran out of juice. Snacking got me through the evening, and Solow happily shared the bounty. Finally, I decided we should go to bed. Solow was at my heels as I carried two candles down the hall to the bedroom. I positioned the flickering lights on my dresser and in semi-darkness, reached for the painting lying on my bed.

"Eeuw!" I grunted and touched the paper again. "It's soaking wet—what the…?"

Solow settled into his bed, unconcerned about my raving suicidal demeanor.

I felt around the paper. The bedspread was soaking wet. How in the world? I held a candle above the center of the bed, and raised it upward. The flame exposed a big wide ceiling bubble extending down a foot or more from where the ceiling should have been. The candle fizzled and went out as cold water dripped on my hand and ran down to my elbow. I found a flashlight in the nightstand drawer and used it to further inspect the ceiling.

"Okay, it's a hole in the roof; now what do I do?" I asked Solow.

He snored like an old man, legs twitching.

Feeling alone and a bit unraveled, my only choice was to call Alicia, since David was out of town and my husband, Marty, had been dead for seventeen years after being run over by an eighteen-wheeler.

Alicia picked up on the second ring.

"So I have this roof problem," I explained, keeping my voice steady, confident Alicia would offer a solution or at least some comforting words. She always did. "I looked at the ceiling with a flashlight and it's just a pin-hole, you know, drip, drip, drip, but the big bubble is full of water. If the ceiling bursts, my room will be flooded."

"That's awful, Jo. What are you going to do?"

"I was hoping you had an idea. Know anyone in the roofing business?"

"Did you know that Marla's younger brother, Melvin, is in construction?

"Where does he live?"

"I think Marla mentioned that Melvin lives with her. Look up Melvin Milford."

"So that means Mary Milford never married?"

"Guess not. But Marla was married and has a daughter and a granddaughter," Alicia said. "She married one of Ernie's cousins, but her husband was in the service and apparently forgot to come home. I think they said he met someone overseas."

"Thanks, Allie. I'll call right away. Bye."

I blew out the second candle and used my flashlight to get to the kitchen drawer where the phonebook lived. Luckily, Melvin's number was in the book. I called.

"Yeah?"

"Melvin? This is Josephine Stuart, I live in Aromas and my roof has a hole in it."

"Yeah?"

"How soon can you fix it?"

"It's pretty stormy right now—gotta' wait for a nicer day."

"But my bed is getting wet…."

"First dry day and I'll come check it out…."

"But, but what do I do in the meantime?"

"Put a tarp on it."

"Good grief, how do I do that?"

Melvin hung up.

Chapter 4

Tuesday morning I opened my eyes to sunshine, birds chirping and a wire mattress coil entombed in my back. I tried to roll over but Solow's weight kept the quilt tight, no room to turn. He finally took the hint from my knee and jumped down to the floor. No wonder my house guests never stayed long. Grandma's old bed in the loft was a back killer.

"Bam, bam, bam," someone knocked hard on the front door.

Solow howled.

I pulled on my robe, scampered down the stairs and opened the front door. A man in his early fifties, wearing overalls and an orange rubber jacket, smiled.

"I'm Mel and I'm here to fix your roof." His blue eyes twinkled.

"I'm sorry I'm not really up and dressed yet—long night, you know. Just go around to the back of the house and you'll see a ladder and a blue tarp on the roof."

"I'll check it out," he winked.

"Oh, and I'm so sorry about your sister, Mary…."

"Yeah, thanks," he said, turning to go.

I raced up to the loft to get dressed, remembering the ghastly evening with no electricity, a soaking wet bed and a ruined painting. I had left the room as-is, and concentrated on covering the hole in the roof. I had pulled on rubber boots and a windbreaker, and sloshed through puddles to the back yard. With the help of my flashlight and a few bolts of lightning, I'd located a blue tarp and a roll of duct tape in the tin shed. I leaned my extension ladder against the house, carried the tarp to the roof top and cautiously crawled onto slippery half-round tiles, all the while holding my breath and praying the wind would not blow me to the ground.

Thunder had kept my heart beating at twice the normal rate, and sweat had run down my face while my bare fingers froze. The tape didn't stick well to wet ceramic tiles and the wind did its best to whip the tarp away from me. In the end, I won the battle. The ten-foot by ten-foot area over my bedroom was covered, including a loose tile I thought might be the problem.

It was late when I'd crawled into Grandma's bed and Solow crept under it. My hair was wet and I couldn't feel my toes, but somehow I'd slept soundly, dreaming about a picnic at the river with Grandma, her famous potato salad and her two Pomeranians.

Mel pounded on the front door.

My mind zoomed into 'real time' as I zipped my zipper, buttoned my buttons and ran to the door to let Mel in. He said he found the trouble, a broken tile near the chimney.

"Not where I spread the tarp?"

"Nope. What happens is the water runs to the lowest spot, collects in the ceiling and stretching it into a bubble. Let's go look at the bubble." I led him to my room where my ruined painting lay on the soggy bed. I quickly grabbed the thick paper and tossed it in the closet. I wasn't in the mood for criticism or sympathy.

Mel just smiled. "Yep, I see the bubble. One wrong move and the whole thing will come down. I noticed you have a garden hose behind the house. I'll bring it in and we'll drain this sucker. I mean, it's going to be okay, trust me."

Once the bubble had been emptied through a garden hose stretched out the window into the back yard, Mel began ripping the ceiling apart and tossing the odd pieces of sheetrock out the window. When there was nothing left to see but the wooden planks of the roof, he helped me take the bed apart and carry the mattress out the back door to the patio. A little bundle of money dropped on the floor.

"I didn't know people really put money under their mattress…." he laughed.

"I do. It's my slush fund for a rainy day. Oh, I guess it *was* a rainy day and I owe you some money. See how well the system works?"

No comment.

Mel went to his pickup truck and came back to my bedroom with two large electric fans which he plugged into action, reminding me of a wind tunnel at the carwash.

"Okay, Ms. Stuart, I'll be on the roof."

"Careful, the tiles are slippery up there…."

"Yeah, thanks." He tipped his backward Giants cap and headed out to his beefed-up black Dodge with giant wheels and lots of chrome. Through the dining room window I watched the nicely-built man pull a large metal toolbox out of the truck bed along with a crowbar and a carpenter's belt full of tools. He disappeared behind the house.

My engine was running on empty—no coffee and no food up to that point—and it was already past noon. I put Mr. Coffee to work and scrounged around the kitchen, eating every fast, sweet and salty junk food I could find.

Ignoring ugly pounding noises overhead, I remembered Solow hadn't had his breakfast. Feeling guilty of pet neglect, I topped off his kibble with a dollop of ice cream. When kitchen chores were finished, I worked on mopping out my bedroom and even cleaned the closet.

Solow watched me from the hall.

"Oh, look at this," I said to Solow. "My old camera from twenty years ago." I opened it up and discovered it was loaded with actual film. The film was probably dead, but I decided I'd finish the roll and have it printed anyway. There might even be some pictures of Marty.

"Smack, screech, bam."

I decided to see how the roof was coming along. Halfway around the house I realized I was still holding the camera. The sun had drifted to the west, but there was still plenty of light so I called up to Mel. He peeked over the roof, looking into the sun, as I pointed the camera and clicked. It would prove to be a smeared action shot of Mel sliding off the roof. His landing was full of cuss words, but he was still breathing.

"Mel? Can you move your arms and legs?" I screamed in terror.

More cuss words. "Yeah," he grimaced. "Everything moves except my ankle."

"Stay there," I shouted as I ran around to the front door and straight to Solow. "I'm sorry, sweetie, but I need your brace. Hold still. Good boy." I raced back to Mel with the doggie brace.

"That looks like the one your dog's wearing…." he muttered, as I carefully placed it around his right ankle. The three Velcro straps weren't long enough so I dashed to the shed and came back with duct tape. After several rounds of tape, the brace was secure.

"I'll help you up," I said, reaching for his right hand, hoping the short brace would allow him to stand on the foot.

"Ouch!" More cuss words. "My wrist hurts…" he moaned.

"Good grief…I mean, I'm so sorry you fell. What do you want me to do now?"

"Don't touch me for starters."

"Okay, stay here; I'll be right back." I ran back to my bedroom, grabbed a plastic coat hanger, stepped on it and broke the thing in three pieces, ignoring Solow's sad eyes and low-grade whimpering. I gathered up a washcloth and one six-inch piece of broken hanger, and ran outside.

Back at Mel's side, I tore three separate six-inch lengths of duct tape using my hands and teeth. Next I wrapped and taped the cloth around Mel's wrist, ignoring his incoherent threats. Laying the plastic over the cloth vertically, I then wrapped the tape horizontally around the wrist. It was a crude looking brace, but Mel didn't fight it. He seemed calmer when I pulled him upright by his left hand, and steadied him as we toddled around the house to the front door.

Solow came out from the bedroom on three legs.

Mel looked down at his ankle. "You actually took his brace?"

"I had to do something. I'll get a new one for Solow; in fact, it's almost five so we'll have to hurry."

"Okay, take me to the hospital after you stop at the vet," he ordered.

I grabbed a coat and purse, said goodbye to Solow and together Mel and I shuffled outside to my truck. The ride to the Veterinary Hospital was beyond quiet. I had already apologized, what more could I say? Apparently Mel had nothing to say so we sped down San Juan Road to Watsonville in silence, straight to Doctor Finley's office. The doctor was getting into his black Porsche as we pulled to a stop in the handicapped parking.

I cut the engine and leaped out of the cab.

The doctor looked startled when I put my hands on his window. He rolled it down.

"Ms. Stuart, can I help you?"

"Solow needs a new brace…."

He looked at his watch. “I’m afraid the doors are locked and....”

“Oh, please, Doctor Finley, Solow’s in pain.”

He climbed out of his car and we walked to the back door of the building. He unlocked the door. I was not invited in so I waited in the shadows for Finley to return. Minutes later, he came back with a box, handed it to me and locked the door.

“Don’t worry about paying me now. We’ll send you a bill,” he said and jumped into his snazzy car.

Ready for more silence, I was surprised when Mel began talking about the condition of my roof.

“So, like I said, the roof is ninety percent fixed. When I can, I’ll come over and install a ceiling for you.”

“Thanks, Mel. I appreciate everything you’ve done so far.” *Except for the cussing*, I thought to myself.

We zigzagged across Watsonville and eventually parked under a streetlight in the hospital parking lot. The stars were out in full force, not a cloud anywhere.

“You stay here. I’ll get help.” I rushed into the building searching for a helpful nurse with a wheelchair. I finally found one at the other end of the building in the emergency room. She rolled a wheelchair out to my truck, collected Mel and rolled him back for x-rays.

“Mel, do you want me to call anyone? Marla? Anyone?”

“Nope.”

“I’ll run some errands while you wait for the doc,” I said, wondering if the x-ray results would end Mel’s career for a while. I went back to my truck and headed over to the one house in Watsonville where I always felt welcome, no matter the time or circumstances.

Alicia opened the door. “Jo, this is a surprise.” She stepped back.

Trigger stepped forward and gave me a hug. His little sheltie dog, Tansey, wagged her tail as she waited for a few pats.

"It's a long story. I just took Mel to the hospital."

"Who's Mel?" She pulled me inside and led me to the kitchen where Ernie stood stirring a pot of something. "Who's Mel?" she repeated.

"Melvin—Mary and Marla's younger brother. He told me to call him Mel. He was fixing my roof when he fell and he's at the hospital and I feel so bad. Oh, Allie, I think it was my fault that he fell…what is that wonderful smell?"

"I have a pork roast in the oven. Can you stay for dinner?"

"Well, yeah, if you're eating soon…."

"Everything's ready. Ernie made the gravy and Trigger set the table. Trigger, please set a place for Auntie Jo. Ernie, the gravy goes in that little white pitcher in the cabinet. Jo, you can take the salad to the table. I'll take the vegetables while Ernie carves the meat."

In all the years of Friday night dinners at the Quintana house, I'd never had anything except authentic Mexican cuisine. This dinner was different, but excellent as always. Alicia just had a knack for perfection. After dinner, she showed me five watercolor paintings she'd finished. I tried not to look envious.

"How is the painting coming along, Jo?"

"I had a pretty good one last night until my bedroom flooded."

Trigger's jaw dropped. "Really, Auntie Jo?"

I nodded and told them the whole story beginning with a leak in the roof, a wet bed, a ruined painting and the sad finale, Mel falling off the roof.

"Allie, would you please call me in the morning when you get up? I need to get started on another painting."

"Don't look so discouraged, Jo, I'll call you."

After good food and comforting words, I left the Quintana's and drove back to the hospital. Mel sat in a plastic chair in the waiting room wearing a big black Velcro-ed boot on his right foot and a matching brace on his right wrist, starring at the floor. But he perked up real fast when I handed him a pork roast sandwich from Alicia.

"Ready to go home?"

"Yeah, back to my little room in the garage," he mumbled.

"Are you saying you live in a garage?"

Mel took a hungry bite out of the sandwich and wiped his chin with his shirt sleeve.

"Along with some other people. It's my sister's place. When I lost my wife and my house—that's a long story—anyway my sisters let me build a room in the detached garage. Trouble is the other half of the garage had already been made into a couple rooms for the Herrera family."

"Why didn't your sisters just ask the family to leave and give the rooms to you?"

He took another juicy bite. "Lots of reasons," he mumbled.

"Like what?"

"Because they like the family much better than me. We've never been real close. Besides, the Herreras have this cute little five-year-old girl. You know how women are…all *goochey, goochey* with kids.

I was tempted to invite Mel to stay at my house for one night, and then I remembered that the bed in the loft was taken because my bed was out of order—squishy wet. My bones ached just thinking about the monsterly uncomfortable bed in the loft. Besides, Mel was a good looking guy close to my age. How would I explain that to David?

Chapter 5

Wednesday morning, I sprang from Grandma's spring-loaded bed in the loft, grabbed my robe and ran down the old wooden stairs to the phone in the living room. Fully awake at that point, I regretted hurrying. What kind of rude person would call so early? It was only seven-thirty—unless it was an emergency. I lifted the receiver.

"Hi, Jo. This is your wake-up call," Alicia said sweetly, knowing full well how much I liked to sleep in.

"Oh yeah, thanks, Allie."

"How's the roofer doing?"

"Okay I guess, but you won't believe where he lives. He lives in Marla's garage. He built a couple little rooms for himself. But that's not all…there's a family of three living in two other little rooms *in* the garage."

She gasped, "How big is this garage?"

"I didn't go in, but from outside, it looks like a normal two-car garage with room for a workshop."

"How big is the house?"

"It's one of those cute little houses in Capitola. Mel said it only has two bedrooms. Maybe Marla will rent out Mary's room."

"Yeah, or rent out a couple closets," Alicia laughed. "I wonder why she needs to rent out her garage. Does Marla need the money or is she just trying to help people who need a place to live?"

"I don't think she needs the money. She drives a new Lexus SUV. She's okay. I think she just wants to help her brother and the young family." Even so, renting out Mary's room sounded like a possibility, especially if another needy person came along.

We hung up, and I let Solow outside for a walk. I watched him through the dining room window as he hobbled through wet grass on three legs, eyeing his nemesis, probably wishing he could indulge in a good cat-chase. Fluffy watched him from her perch on a fence post ten yards away, completely unconcerned.

Once I was showered, dressed and fed, I let Solow into the house and began concentrating on subject matter for my next painting. I thought about painting ideas as I folded clothes from the dryer, loaded the dishwasher and walked to the end of the driveway for the newspaper. When all the chores were done, I sat at the dining room table, holding my chin up with one hand, flipping magazine pages with the other.

Finally, I slapped the magazine closed and began taping watercolor paper to a board, hoping an idea would float to the surface of my anxious brain. I thought about the most famous paintings in the world and the artists who'd painted them. But those pictures had been painted with oil paints, and many were on the dark side. I wanted to paint something light, full of life, fresh and colorful.

I thumbed through my mail and discovered a travel magazine. Why the travel company wasted their advertising money on me I would never know, but several scenes in the booklet were inspiring. I chose the Norwegian fiords, featuring colorful pointy roofed houses and buildings lined up at the edge of a deep ultramarine blue waterway, nothing like the sinister silver-grey water that had swept poor Mary away.

David had said that Mary's footprints faced the land, not the sea. I could think of only one reason why a person would turn their back to the ocean. Did she take a selfie, or was someone else taking her picture? If it was someone else, why didn't they report what happened? Unless the person wanted it to happen. I shivered. Marla came to mind. She'd expressed sadness in the days following the murder of her sister, but after a week and a half, she seemed to be back to normal.

I tried to picture myself losing a sister, but since I was an only child I thought about losing Alicia. It was too devastating to imagine. My eyes watered just thinking about it. I picked up the phone and dialed.

"Hi, Jo. I thought you'd be engrossed in your painting...."

"I finally found a picture I want to paint, but I started thinking about poor Mary. I think someone took a picture of her standing out there on the cliff."

"That seems possible," she said.

"Allie, I just had a thought—what if I stayed at Marla's house a couple days. Maybe I could look around a bit...."

"Jo, are you nuts? You can't just insert yourself into someone's house."

"I know the perfect way and it's all true. I'll tell Marla that my bed is soaking wet from the leak in the roof and the bed in the loft is killing my back. I'll just ask for a couple nights rest while my mattress dries out."

"Are you going to snoop around my house too?" Alicia snapped. "I was there at the cliffs painting that day."

"Yeah, right next to me...besides, murder isn't in your makeup."

"I'm glad you didn't ask for my opinion...." she said.

"I know what you think about it, but I just have to find out who took a picture of Mary. Okay, now that that's settled, I need to paint."

We hung up and I took a break for lunch. I popped a burrito in the microwave and dialed Marla's number taken from my list of art class members.

"Marla, hi! This is Josephine…Josephine Stuart from Kati's watercolor class and Sonia's yoga…."

"Yes, pardon me, now I know who you are. I was taking a little nap…."

"Speaking of naps, I haven't had a good night's sleep for two days. I don't know if Mel told you…."

"As a matter of fact, he said something about fixing your roof. He wasn't very ha…."

"Yeah, anyway, my mattress is soaked and I'm afraid that mold has set in."

"Already?"

"Probably a new fast-growing strain. So I was wondering if you had an extra bed I could rent."

"You want to rent Mary's bed?" She sneezed.

"Well, to tell you the truth, Marla, I need a place to stay until my mattress dries."

"Josephine, I would never turn anyone away, but the sheets need to be laundered…." She sneezed again.

"I'll wash the sheets when I get there. No problem. Thanks, Marla. See you around eight?"

"Actually, I won't be back from my photography class in Santa Cruz."

"No problem, just leave a key under the door mat." We hung up.

That was the moment when an idea came to me. I picked up the phone and dialed Alicia. Why hadn't I thought of it sooner? Alicia's house sat less than a hundred feet from the edge of Drew Lake, a picturesque scene with green hills lined up behind still blue water. Wild geese, ducks and cormorants hung out on the little beach near the Quintana boat dock. White Herron and Blue Herron dove for fish among the reeds.

I called and Alicia was open to the idea that we would paint the lake together. After all, she had giant windows across the back of the house facing the water. She said she just needed another hour to finish El Capitan in her Yosemite picture that she'd copied from a vacation photograph.

After mural-painting professionally for fifteen years, I had begun to doubt my artistic ability. On second thought, the clients I'd worked for were usually very happy with my artwork. Maybe it was just watercolor techniques that didn't agree with me. I hoped some of Alicia's "happy confidence" would give me a better attitude.

I packed a small suitcase for myself and a doggie bed and some kibble for Solow. I put my paints and paper in the truck bed, and called David to let him know that I wouldn't be home until Thursday. He sounded disappointed.

As I drove toward Watsonville, the sky darkened north of Santa Cruz. Ten minutes later, clouds were galloping south into the Watsonville area, threatening to blow away a rainbow arching itself over little farm houses surrounded by hundreds of acres of green vegetables. It would have made a beautiful painting, but I didn't stop until we reached Alicia's house.

Alicia held the front door open.

Solow and I ran across the street to the Quintana property. Thunder rumbled overhead and a cool gust of wind tried to unbalance me. The watercolor paper flapped but I held tight. We made it through the doorway just before rain drops pelted the neighborhood. Solow hip-hopped into the house on three legs and sniffed Tansey, his only dog friend with shorter legs than his own.

The lake was a distant blur as my friend and I stared out the dining room window through torrential rain.

"Care for a hot cup of tea?" Alicia asked.

"Sure, what else can we do?" I groaned. "Tea sounds good."

"Maybe the storm will pass through quickly...."

"Right, and I'll finish a painting of the lake, and Mary's killer will give himself up. Oh for a perfect world."

"It's not that bad, Jo. We can paint a still life. I have bananas, oranges, grapes, lemons and apples."

"You're right, let's not waste good paint-time."

Alicia spread newspaper over her dining room table and we set up our painting equipment on the paper. We collaborated on setting up the fruit, organizing it on a wooden cutting board, trying to control roll-away oranges. Short of a 6.5 earthquake, the fruit was finally stationary.

My background color was going to be a deep purple, almost black, so I began with fruit and ended by carefully working the dark color around the subject matter. By six o'clock my picture was finished and I was satisfied. Alicia finished earlier, giving her time to putter around the kitchen making enchiladas. I hated to impose, but decided to stay for dinner and drive straight to Capitola at eight.

The twelve-mile drive to Capitola was wildly wet, my wipers barely able to keep up with the downpour. I leaned into the windshield, hoping to locate the white line. My nervous breath fogged the glass, making things even more difficult. The deluge let up a bit as I rolled into the "Jewel" neighborhood of Capitola, rightly named because of streets like Emerald, Ruby, Pearl and Jade.

Marla's house had a perfect view of Jade Street Park. I pulled up to the curb behind her SUV and cut the engine. Parked in front of the SUV was a real classic, the cutest little blue Porsche 911.

The porch light blinked on. Darn! Marla was home. How could I snoop around with her home? There was nothing left for us to do but go inside. Picking up on my mood, Solow reluctantly followed me up the sidewalk. I heard music off to the right, coming from the garage area. Solow veered off the walkway and headed across the lawn toward the garage. I called him. He stopped, marked a birdbath and came back to me.

Marla stood at the open front door, watching us with a knitted lap blanket wrapped around her shoulders. She greeted me and promptly sneezed. She showed me to a seat in the living room, gave Solow a timid pat on his pointy head and sneezed. She honked her nose in a tissue and sneezed again.

"Sorry, Josephine, I tried to call you but I guess you weren't home. I'm not sure…ah—ah—choo…if it's allergy or flu."

The "flu" word smacked me like an ice-cold shower.

"Did you come down with it today?" I asked sweetly, feeling like I wanted to dash out of the stuffy room into the cool night air and race home to Grandma's deadly mattress.

"Yes, today, but I'll be fine. What happened to your dog?" she asked with a forced smile, the type used by people who dislike dogs.

"A UPS truck hit him, but he'll be fine, just cracked a couple toes."

"Oh, that's nice. Ah-choo!"

"I'll just go put my suitcase in the bedroom." I stood up.

"First door on the, ah, ah, right. Ah-choo!" Marla pointed toward the hall.

Solow and I entered the hallway, turned right and found our room full of camera equipment, piles of yarn, a rock-rolling machine, a large collection of colored feathers, a sewing machine, beads of every color and size for jewelry making and six large plastic tubs stacked to the ceiling labeled "Christmas Decorations."

"Ah-choo."

I turned around. "Oh, Marla, didn't see you there."

"This was Mary's room. As a way to honor her memory, I decided I would use it as a craft room. She loved crafts. I'll move the fishing pole so you can get to the bed. I've been home all day washing sheets and such."

"Thank you, I'm so grateful for a dry place to sleep. You wouldn't believe my other bed. It's so old it has metal coils and sags in the middle."

Marla blew into a tissue. "Now you have a dry bed and your own TV," she chuckled.

I looked around the well-organized, full to the brim room and spied an old black and white Emerson TV, its guts replaced with a fish tank and a bunch of shiny little fish. I yawned and said goodnight.

"But Josephine, it's only nine o'clock. Why don't you watch the game shows with me?"

"Ah, yeah, I'll join you in a minute. I just want to unpack." Marla walked out the door, honking into her tissue. I looked around for Solow and finally found him curled up under the bed. He wouldn't come out and I didn't blame him. I imagined creepy little flu bugs, all slimy green, chasing after us. All things considered, I decided to live out of my suitcase since there was no room anywhere for my things and our stay with Marla would be as brief as possible.

After an evening of game shows and trying to keep my distance from Ms. Andromeda Strain wearing sweats and a hot water bottle, I finally hit the sack.

"Ouch!" The "sack" turned out to be a twin bed—the ugly twin of my Grandmother's saggy coil bed from you-know-where. My phone rang. By the time I rolled out of bed and foraged through my purse for the cell phone, it had stopped ringing. But it showed David's number so I called him.

"Josie, where are you, honey?"

"I decided to spend the night at Marla's house in Capitola."

"You know you can always stay here…."

I laughed. "I know, but I thought Marla might appreciate some company now that her sister was murdered." I sat on the side of the bed eyeing a camera on the desk against the far wall. It looked like a digital point-and-shoot. I worked my way around boxes of books and a basket of yarn, picked up the camera and poked the *on* button.

"What was that?" he said. "Sounded like a camera."

"You guessed it—just putting away my camera."

"Josie, I smell an ulterior motive here. The unsolved murder wouldn't have anything to do with your visit, would it?"

"I just thought I should be here for Marla, with a death in the family and all, in case she needs help with anything…like laundry and stuff." I could tell by his sarcastic voice he wasn't buying it. "I'll see you tomorrow. Goodnight, my sweet prince."

"Goodnight, my lady, and stay out of trouble!" he laughed.

What kind of trouble would I get into? I could barely roll over on Mary's saggy mattress. The room was dark and quiet except for the sound of someone walking across the patio and knocking over a ceramic pot, by the sound of it. By the time I crawled out of the contrary bed and peeked out the window, the person was gone. I climbed back in bed and pulled the blanket up over my chin.

Nightmares ensued. I was back on the Capitola cliff clinging to a string attached to a kite, being manipulated by someone in the shadows. A gull screamed. Someone peddled by on a bike. I tried to see who it was, but the string broke and I started to fall.

Chapter 6

Thursday morning, seven o'clock, Marla poked her head in the bedroom door to tell me she was leaving for work. Still in an inert state of slumber, my body jerked and I slowly opened my eyes.

"I'm sorry, what did you say?" I rubbed my eyes and sat up in bed.

"I'm off to work—that's all."

"Where do you work?" I had no idea she had a job.

"I'm a social worker in Hollister. Anything you need, Josephine, before I go?"

"You drive all the way to Hollister?"

"I used to work in Santa Cruz County, but I had a little problem with too many traffic tickets. But I like San Benito County too."

I wished Marla a good day as she left the room, and made a mental note not to ride with her under any circumstances.

"Ouch!" I put my feet to the floor. My body hurt from one end to the other, probably from being trapped in a low spot in the middle of the mattress all night. Solow, on the other hand, looked rested. He yawned and stretched as I pulled on my robe. We trundled down the hall, cut through the living room-dining room area and discovered a bright yellow kitchen decorated with hens and roosters of every sort.

I pushed the hen and rooster patterned curtains open, giving me a view of the fenced back yard and one side wall of the garage. The lawn had puddles everywhere and the sky looked ready to deliver more of the same. I poured kibble into Solow's bowl, but he decided he needed to go outside before eating.

As soon as I opened the door for my gimpy boy I realized he was on another cat chase. This time it was a black and white kitten. Solow hip-hopped on three legs after the young cat, barking his head off. Suddenly the kitten stopped, turned around and hissed. Solow was dumbfounded and ran back to the kitchen door, tail tucked, howling to be let in.

As I opened the door, a little girl came out the side door of the garage and crossed the patio.

"Senorita, shhh, my mama ees sleeping. She does work very late."

"Sorry," I said as I let Solow into the kitchen.

From the window I watched the little girl scoop up the cat, carry it into the garage and shut the door. She reminded me of the little girl Robert's mother described, talking to Mary at the cliffs, which reminded me I needed to check out Marla's camera. Side-tracked again, Solow watched as I sat on the bed flipping through a photo album I found under a pile of books. The pictures were not recent and therefore not helpful, so I carefully put the album back where I found it.

When I finished making up the bed, I sidled over to Mary's desk where I examined the digital camera and began pushing buttons and turning things. I looked for pictures from the recent past.

"Oops!" Click, flash. "Now how do I erase this stupid picture of my feet?" I said to Solow. He slunk under the bed. I finally gave up, admitting for the millionth time that my gene-pool lacked all traces of the techie-gene. I only knew how to perform the most basic tasks with my own camera, used mainly to record walls—before and after I painted murals on them.

I foraged through a couple drawers in the small desk that doubled as a night stand and found paper and pencil, enabling me to write a 'thank you' note to Marla. I tried to ignore the leather bound journal in that same drawer, but, alas, I couldn't stop myself from confiscating it. I didn't open the book, just tossed it into my bag next to my pajamas as if it landed there by accident.

Solow followed me into the kitchen, watching me as I placed the thank you note against a ceramic rooster napkin holder on the kitchen counter.

The hen and chicks clock on the wall indicated it was eight o'clock. My stomach growled. Rather than hunt for food in Marla's fridge, I hauled Solow and our luggage out to the truck and headed into Watsonville.

My pickup jerked to a stop in front of the Cowboy Café. I instructed Solow briefly on passenger seat etiquette, such as no drooling or chewing. He put his head down and closed his eyes as I climbed out of the cab. The restaurant was humming, no empty tables anywhere, so I stepped over to the counter and ordered an egg, bacon and bean burrito to go.

Someone tapped me on the shoulder.

I twirled around. "Claudia, are you here for breakfast?"

"Yes, Vick and I have a table right over there." She pointed across the room to a gentleman wearing black skinny jeans, black polyester shirt and a shiny blue vest. He smiled and waved.

"Why don't you join us, Josephine?"

"Okay, thanks, I'll have them serve my order at your table. I turned back to the counter and made my wishes known while Claudia tramped across the room, moving her hips this way and that between the tables, showing no signs of a sprained ankle, all the way back to Vick. I wondered if they had a "romantic thing" going. The only way to find out was to join them for breakfast.

Vick's cologne accosted me half-way across the room. I wiggled my way between table after table in a room full of loud chatter, all the way to a bank of large windows and the smiling couple.

Slick Vick stood and pulled a chair out for me.

"Do you two come here often?" I asked.

"Oh no," Claudia giggled, looking like a sixty-five-year-old blushing school girl. "Vick happened to be eating alone. I walked in and he kindly invited me to share his table, and now we are a lovely threesome."

My seat faced the window. A new rain storm added water to old puddles in the parking lot while gusty winds set a distant row of eucalyptus swaying to the beat of Michael Jackson's *Thriller*. At least I didn't have to worry about Solow becoming over-heated while sleeping in the cab. I could relax, enjoy my breakfast and save a couple bites for my buddy.

"How have you been, Josephine?" Claudia asked.

"Frustrated! I'm trying to create a collection of watercolor paintings for the Art Festival in Aromas, but so far I only have two paintings suitable for framing. You see, my roof had a hole in it, my bed flooded and my grandma's bed was too uncomfortable so I stayed overnight at Marla's last night."

Vick watched the rain and Claudia yawned.

"So what have you two been up to?" I took another bite of my burrito.

Claudia said, "Speaking of the Art Festival, did you know that Kati is taking Mary's spot, the booth everyone wants? I'm not saying Kati wants it that bad, just sayin.'" Claudia scraped the last runny bite of her eggs Benedict onto her fork.

"I didn't know Kati got Mary's spot," Vick grumped. "I wanted it myself, but I guess I'm too late." He stabbed a bite of ham with his fork.

"So what's so good about that spot anyway?" I asked.

"Well," Claudia looked at me as if I'd just arrived on planet Earth, "Karen had it before Mary and she sold sooo many oil paintings. Actually, Mary did very well last year and the year before with her knitted hats and scarves…."

Vick swallowed a bite of sausage. "Wasn't Karen run over by a hit-and-run driver?"

"Yes." Claudia shivered. "Terrible, terrible. That was three years ago."

"That booth seems to have bad luck attached to it," I said, and swigged down some coffee. "Did you guys know that Mary had a boyfriend?"

"No!" Claudia's eyes were extra big behind thick lenses.

"Everybody knew that," Vick smirked. "I'm an old friend of Kirby's. Buzz, Kirby and I joined the service together right out of high school. Kirby used to hang out with Mary because he knew she didn't want to get married. No pressure, that sort of thing." Vick wiped toast crumbs and butter off his chin with his napkin.

I finished eating my breakfast burrito except for about three bites. When the waitress came around with the bill, I asked for a doggie box. She opened her mouth to say something, but good-waitress-standards must have stopped her. Her forever smile faded as she headed back to the congested kitchen for a box.

Claudia and Vick glanced at my plate.

"This is a little treat for my dog, Solow," I explained. "He's waiting for me in my truck."

"How sweet of you," Claudia purred.

Vick chimed in, "Must be a miniature…."

"Actually, he's a fifty-pound French Basset. I'm counting calories for him."

I thought about breakfast at the Cowboy Café as I drove home. Vick sure had a friendly touch when Claudia dropped her napkin on the floor. He retrieved it, letting his hand rest on hers for a second as he handed it to her. She batted her eyes and thanked him. Curious to me was the fact that they sat kitty-corner to each other instead of using opposite chairs. Maybe retired folks spent their time sparking each other. Maybe "oldies" had more fun than the working generation.

I parked in front of my house next to Mel's black Dodge pickup and helped Solow out of his seat, placing him on the ground gently. He did the three-legged hustle up to the front door and I let him in.

"Ewe! I smell mold." It didn't bother Solow but it sure bothered me. I opened doors and windows, turned up the furnace and tracked down mold locations with a spray bottle of chlorine bleach. My bedroom ceiling dripped bleach for the rest of the day.

Thank goodness it was only ten-thirty and I had the rest of the day to paint. I positioned my board, paper, paints and brushes on the dining room table, hoping an idea for a painting would strike.

Solow barked.

The door bell rang.

I answered the door. Probably some guy selling solar panels. I prepared myself to say "no" right away and not listen to the blah, blah, blah sales pitch.

"Oh, deputies, what's new?"

Officer Sayer followed Officer Lund into the house. Lund wrinkled her pointy nose like she just smelled something detestable.

Sayer ignored the moldy chlorine smell. "Ms. Stuart, we think you might be the closest person to the Milford murder."

I took a step back and sat down. The rocker rocked gently.

"What I mean is, you know everyone in the painting class and you were the first person to report seeing a red sweater in the surf. We're wondering if you know anything else, anything new?"

The rocker sped up. "I've asked around here and there, but nothing new so far." Did they think of me as 'a person of interest' in the case? Why me? I didn't know anything.

Deputy Lund's eyes drilled into mine. "Do you know if anyone else was on that path, anyone with a cell phone or a camera?"

"No, I told you I saw a person on a bike and a little dog running loose…that's all." I thought about Robert's mother seeing a little girl speaking Spanish to Mary, but kept quiet. She was reported to be young, like the little girl living in Marla's garage. If by chance the little girls were one, living at Marla's, and I tattled on her, her family might have to leave their undocumented half of the garage. Besides, how could a little girl push a hundred and fifty pound woman off a cliff?

Sayer handed me his card.

Lund cocked her head to one side and gave me a squinty-eyed look of disbelief. And then there was the sweet sound of a cruiser crunching down my gravel driveway to Otis Road. They were leaving Aromas, and so was I. Painting would have to wait. I needed a walk on the beach, the one nearest the cliff where Mary did her swan dive.

I left Solow sleeping, enjoying his mid-morning nap, and pointed my pickup toward the Pacific Ocean—Capitola in particular. I knew all about Capitola and its fabulous beaches, sunsets, restaurants and shops. But more recently I knew about how dangerous its cliffs could be, especially at high tide in stormy weather. Mary was a great example of that!

Capitola was surrounded by ocean on its western side, Santa Cruz to the north, Soquel to the east and Aptos to the south. The Capitola Wharf dated back to 1850, and the town was built on the location of an Indian village that existed for more than a thousand years. That was part of the attraction for me. I could practically feel the history just by looking at the 150-year-old 'six sisters' houses,' six slim, hip-to-hip, pointy roofed, well-kept two-story houses just yards from the beach.

Too bad it wasn't a day to enjoy the village, no time for window shopping. I parked in the lot near the cliffs overlooking the wharf and a long curved beach, locked the truck and stuffed my phone, wallet and keys into my Levi pockets. After zipping up my sweatshirt, I scrambled down to the infamous path where Mary had spent her last moments on earth. Standing on the footpath facing the ocean I looked for the exact spot where Mary had stood, and searched for her foot prints. The yellow tape Robert talked about was gone and so were any clear prints. It looked like quite a few dogs had passed through that area. I looked over the side. The tide was out. Giant rocks leaned against the base of the cliff, dry as powder, looking harmless in the sunlight.

I followed the path southeast, toward a long steep set of wooden stairs that took me down to the beach. White sand glistened that beautiful winter day making it a great opportunity for beach combing, a favorite activity for many locals. At the bottom of the stairs, I turned right and walked in a westerly direction, head down, eyes trained on the cluttered sand. Battered and torn household goods, including a kitchen sink, were wrapped in long strands of kelp and sealed with seagull droppings. Twisted and tangled tree branches were strewn over the beach, sent there by a ferocious ocean gone wimpy. The sad scene didn't surprise me, considering the fact that several homes along the California coast had slid into the ocean during the last storm.

As I shuffled through the sand, I gladly soaked up the sun, enjoying the sparkling water, soaring gulls and little faraway fishing boats over a flat blue ocean.

Two little boys wearing matching blue jackets tussled in the sand a couple yards away from their mother who'd fallen asleep stretched out on a beach towel, an open book covering her face.

Further down the beach, a man walked his beefy dog on a leash. The dog growled as we passed each other. The man tightened up on the leash.

After a lengthy walk to the end of the sand and back, I notice the boys were fighting over an object glinting in the cool sunlight. I moseyed over to see what they had.

"Thanks, guys, for finding my phone," I whispered, as I leaned down and grabbed it away from four grubby little hands.

"Mommy, she took my phone!"

"It was my phone first!"

"Quiet, you two! You don't own a phone." The book stayed on her face.

"Mommeee!"

"Liam, Lamar, hush! Mama needs her rest."

I dropped the silver phone into my pocket, did a fast walk to the wooden staircase and hustled up fifty or a hundred steps to the truck. Warm and panting, I climbed into the cab and shut the door. The cracked, dinged and smashed cell phone had my full attention. I barely noticed a tall, muscular blond standing between his Jeep and my truck, changing from wetsuit into Levis.

I brushed sand off the little glass window with my fingers, wishing the phone would wake up and reveal to me what it had seen that day on the cliff—assuming it was the right camera-phone. I pushed on the cracked screen expecting nothing and nothing was all I got, except for an idea. My friend, Robert, from the grocery store had once bragged about his techie friend who was very talented when it came to computers and such.

"Full throttles ahead, Sir Mazda!" I said to my trusty pickup, as Christmas music filled the cab. A little white cattle dog ran out from behind my truck. I revved the engine and carefully backed out of the parking space, reminded that I should bring Solow to Capitola for a run on the beach some day. Actually, it wasn't always possible to walk along the cliffs. It would have to be at low-tide.

Day dreaming about what might be inside the phone, I drove through Capitola Village and entered Highway One. All the way to Watsonville I could barely contain my excitement. I parked and hurried into the grocery store where Robert worked at many jobs—cashier, stocker and produce manager. I found him in the produce aisle stacking cantaloupes.

"Josephine, got some nice strawberries today…."

"That's nice, but I have a question for you. What's the name of that techie friend you told me about? I think you called him an Aussie."

"I know who you're talking about. Jake Bigfoot, I mean, Leadfoot. That's a joke…it's Jake Leadfoot. You have a computer problem?"

"This phone might be harboring a clue in the Mary Milford case." I handed him the phone. Robert turned it over and over in his hands, eyebrows pushing together.

He shook his head slowly, side to side. "What do you expect to get out of this piece of junk?"

"Hopefully, a picture of Mary…."

"If any one can do it, Jake's your man." He handed the phone back to me. "Do you want strawberries, or not?"

"Sure, I'll pick up a few things since I'm here. Where does Jake live? I'll need a phone number."

"Capitola; he has an apartment in the village down by the river." Robert scribbled seven numbers on the back of a small sale sign for organic beets. "Here's the phone number."

The minute I got home I called Jake. He sounded unfocused, like a guy taking a phone call while repairing two computers at the same time. After I explained how I got his number we were able to agree on a meeting—his place, Friday at one o'clock.

My heart raced. What if Jake couldn't find anything–-pictures or numbers? I knew I shouldn't think that way. I should be optimistic, but the phone was such a mess. It was a lucky find, but maybe it had nothing to do with Mary, just someone's old phone. After a long talk with myself I was finally able to let it go. What will be, will be and all that rot.

Someone knocked on the back door, pushed it open and walked in. Tall and handsome, David smiled his killer smile. He was there, I was putty and the phone was forgotten.

Chapter 7

Friday morning I woke up in a sweat. I dreamt David found Mary's journal in my room and he called Marla to rat on me. Why did I have to dream such a thing after a lovely evening with wonderful David? Because of guilt for taking the journal and anxiety because I had yet to find the time to read the book. I could wait no longer. Twenty hours had passed and I had not changed my mind. A killer was still on the loose and the world would be better off when he was found.

I had to read Mary's journal, regardless of my feelings of guilt.

If I had the right "touch" and was really lucky—or psychic—I should be able to open Mary's book exactly on an important page. I closed my eyes, tried to feel psychic and opened the book near the middle. She talked about her sciatic pain and her scaboria rectamolia or some such thing. She mentioned she had another two-hundred dollars for "the fund," and said she wished she could move to New Zealand.

Nothing on that page seemed important so I flipped back to the beginning, dated fourteen months ago. Three pages later, the Herrera family moved into the garage—Mom, Dad and five-year-old Laurita. Mary talked about her responsibility to take care of the family, but many pages later I still don't know why she thinks they're her responsibility.

Completely engrossed in the journal, I had forgotten my back ache from sleeping on Grandma's death-trap of a mattress. I even forgot to give Solow his breakfast, and mine for that matter. I put the book down.

Solow thumped his tail on the floor as I prepared enough bacon and eggs for both of us. It was another meal with my dog instead of David. Why didn't I marry my wonderful neighbor? Maybe I needed my independence a little longer? I had thought about it many times, especially those times when David hinted around the subject, hoping I'd listen to a marriage proposal.

Once the breakfast dishes were taken care of, I had to decide between Mary's journal and painting a watercolor masterpiece. Only two weeks remained until Alicia and I would hang our paintings on the grange wall. I wrenched my mind away from the journal and succumbed to the pressure to paint. I began with a picture of Solow as he napped. Long ago my art teachers had warned their students not to choose warm cuddly or cute subjects. Fortunately, Solow fell into the ruggedly handsome category.

Just before noon the phone rang. I put my brush in water and answered it.

"Hi, Jo; are you painting today?" Alicia asked.

"Yeah, in fact, I'm almost finished with a picture of Solow. I think it's the best painting I ever…."

"Jo, I called to tell you that I ran into Marla today at the grocery store…."

"That's nice. I think I'll try to finish another picture this after…."

"Jo, Marla told me something interesting."

All of a sudden I was listening.

"She said that Mary crashed her car two years ago. Guess who she crashed into."

"I have no idea," I yawned.

"The Herrera family! She t-boned the driver's side and Mr. Herrera is paralyzed. He gets around in a wheel chair. Mrs. Herrera supports the family working in a convalescent hospital in Capitola. Marla said that was why Mary had the garage apartment built and insisted the family move there and stay for free. She was always giving them gifts and groceries. And she was like a grandma to the little girl."

"Didn't the Herreras have family…?"

"No, they were new in this country. They had just bought an old car."

"So they were probably undocumented, no license or insurance?"

"That's right. Marla told me she plans to let the family stay as long as they need to. I think she's fond of the little girl. She told me that the mother came across the border to have an "American baby" and then went back to Tijuana. A couple years later, she married Pedro, the father, and the family crossed the border and headed north. They'd only been in Santa Cruz County a few days when Mary hit their car.

Alicia knew what it was like to be a stranger in America. She'd lived in Mexico selling chewing gum on the streets of Tijuana at a very young age. Eventually she was adopted by an American couple, earned a bachelors degree in art and married Biology Professor Ernie Quintana. Ten years ago they produced a wonderful son, Trigger.

"Have you painted anything today?" I asked Alicia.

"Yes, I got up early and painted the sunrise over the lake."

"How many paintings so far?"

"Eight. Don't worry, Jo, you'll catch up."

We hung up.

I glanced at the kitchen wall clock.

"Solow, it's already twelve-thirty and I'm supposed to be in Capitola in half an hour."

Solow opened one eye, sighed and went back to sleep.

I checked my purse to make sure the broken phone was in it—it was. I slid the purse strap over my shoulder, grabbed a sweater and hurried over to the truck. My sweet Mazda kicked gravel for fifty yards, all the way to Otis Road. I drove through the tiny town of Aromas, shot down San Juan Road between thousands of acres of lettuce and berries basking in the winter sun and entered Highway One heading north.

Twelve miles later, I left Highway One and all traces of sunshine. Exiting into the backdoor of Capitola, I quickly pulled off my sunglasses and leaned into the windshield, straining to see the road ahead as thick fog enveloped everything in front of me. The narrow streets and quaint shops were barely visible, just a few clusters of red geraniums visible here and there. Palm trees and ocean waves faded into the milky air. The mysterious looking streets were nearly empty, allowing me a quick ride through town. I parked two blocks away from Jake's apartment, the closest parking available, and hustled over to his building. The two-story, turn-of-the-century stucco apartment building faced Soquel Creek. The creek rushed by, seeming to be in a hurry to empty itself into the Pacific Ocean two blocks away.

I found the door with the right numbers next to it and rang the door bell. Immediately, there came a shout from inside.

"Mind yer own bizo, bloke!"

After a moment's hesitation, I mustered up some courage, turned the knob and let myself in. My eyes slowly adjusted to a room lit by electronics. The most light came from a computer screen in the far corner of the room, a room that obviously served as living room, dining room, kitchen and bedroom. The narrow bed had not been made and dirty dishes filled the little kitchen sink. A tall body sat in a chair with little wheels.

Hunched over a computer screen, the young man turned in his chair and apologized for his rude cockatoo, the big white bird across the room balancing on one foot atop his cage.

“That’s okay, Mr. Bigfoot, I mean Leadfoot,” I said, “I should have known it was a bird.”

“I’m glad that’s all the bloke said,” Jake laughed. “It could have been bloody worse. Call me Jake.” We shook hands.

Jake tossed his head of shoulder-length straight brown and blond hair out of his youthfully smooth tanned face. A small earring hoop sparkled, then disappeared as hair fell forward again. I guessed Jake to be in his early twenties, possibly six-foot-four or five, judging by his large sandaled feet.

“So, I have this phone…” I said, tugging the smashed-up thing out of my purse. A small section of glass was missing. I made a mental note to be careful when poking around in the old fake-gator bag. I handed the phone to Jake.

“Kicked the bucket, looks like! Who did it?”

“Maybe it was the same person who pushed Mary Milford off a cliff into the ocean.”

“Jees, are you kidding?” He turned the phone over and over in his hands.

“I wish I was kidding. Mary was a nice lady. What’s the prognosis on this puppy?”

“Jees, I don’t know; looks like it’s not worth a Zack. I’ll do what I can…might have to take it apart….” He seemed lost in thought. “Give me your number and I’ll ring you up when I know more about her.” His eyes shone like he was seven years old, and it was Christmas morning.

"Jake, I'm especially interested in any photographs taken in the last few weeks. If you see any signs of anything interesting, please don't tell anyone about this but me. Here's my card."

"Okay, nobody else….no worries. She'll be right if I can do her. I'm stoked."

"Thank you, Jake; see you later." I opened the front door. Jake didn't look up, so I left quietly. The last thing I wanted to do was break his concentration.

I purposely drove through Capitola using the Esplanade so I would have a close-up view of the ocean on my right and the six sisters housing on my left.

My phone rang. I pulled over to the side of the road and answered it.

"Josie, where are you?"

"Oh, hi David; I'm driving home from Capitola…."

"Alicia called me to remind you that we're going over there for dinner at seven. Did you remember?"

"Um, sort of. I've been kinda' busy. Thanks for the reminder. Can you pick me up at six-thirty?"

"Sure, Josie, see you later." We hung up and I drove on to Marla's house where I parked along the curb behind a white pickup truck. Marla's SUV wasn't around so I walked to the side of the house, through the gate and down the path to the side door of the garage. I opened the door a titch. An inner-wall stretched end-to-end in front of me with a door on the right and one on my left.

I stepped up to the closest door, the one on my right and knocked. The door cracked open a tiny bit. A small girl with large dark eyes, wearing her mother's black t-shirt peeked out.

"Mama not here." She slammed the door.

I knocked on the second door. Mel opened it wearing sweats, one black boot, one wrist brace and a three-day black beard that went well with his shiny black crew cut. Two nerdy young guys—one tall, one short—played an electronic game on Mel's TV.

"Josephine, what are you....?"

"Hi, Mel. I came by to get your truck keys so I can get it back to you."

"Yeah, that would be good. By the way, do you have homeowner's insurance?"

"Yes I do, and I'll give them a call as soon as I get home. Thanks for reminding me. Do you have your hospital bill handy?"

"I'll get it for you." A moment later he handed me the keys and a packet full of paperwork. "I hear you're pretty good at solving murder mysteries; is that true?"

I looked over at the two guys completely engrossed in their game.

"Well," I blushed, "I've had pretty good luck at it in the past. Actually, I have a guy named Jake looking into a suspicious phone I found at the bottom of the cliff where Mary landed."

Mel's eyes were big. "No kidding? Are we talking about that crazy Aussie, Jake Leadfoot?"

"Yeah. How did you know?"

"Everybody knows he's the go-to man when you need serious stuff done."

I dropped the keys in my purse and ducked out the door before I could tell Mel any more of my secrets. One quick stop at the taco drive-thru and I was on my way home.

Friday afternoon traffic was the worst, probably Christmas shoppers. I set the radio on my favorite oldies station, the only one of its kind still in existence, and tried to plot out my next painting. What if I painted Fluffy? No, I couldn't paint her, I would probably make her look like a killer feline with fangs and fire shooting out of her nostrils.

I turned up the radio. My hands automatically beat time on the steering wheel to "Rockin' Around the Christmas Tree."

I could paint marigolds growing in my window boxes under the front windows of my house, except the plants were droopy, frost-bitten and full of bugs. I should do something about that. I was so lost in thought I almost missed my Riverside exit into Watsonville. Two guys in a white pickup beeped at me as I made a quick lane-change. Halfway to San Juan Road, the white truck passed me. I followed it all the way to Aromas and up my driveway.

Sitting in my truck for a couple minutes, I watched the two guys check out Mel's souped up pickup. I climbed out of my truck and slammed the door. They stomped out their cigarettes in the dirt and turned to see who was there.

"We're here for the truck."

"Who sent you?"

The tall one cocked his head. "Mel, of course."

"Okay. I have the keys." I heard Solow barking inside as I rummaged through my purse, finally pulling out the set of keys Mel had given me.

The shorter, thicker fellow stepped up and took them. They went to their respective trucks and revved the engines.

I hurried into the house before the gravel started to fly.

Solow was having a barking fit—who were those guys?

I stopped to give him an ear rub and sooth his nerves. Once Solow was relaxed, I punched the play button on the answering machine in the kitchen and listened to Mom asking me to come to Sunday dinner, Alicia asking if I had a couple tomatoes I could bring to dinner and Marla telling me I'd left my umbrella at her house.

It was all good news. I hadn't seen Mom and Dad in weeks, I did have two tomatoes in the fridge for Alicia, and the umbrella was just the excuse I needed to snoop around Marla's house a little more. But first on my list was a call to Barry, my insurance agent. I punched in his number. He asked for a message—I left him one.

Three painting hours were left before David would be picking me up for our dinner date at Alicia's. Not wanting to waste a minute of it, I quickly spread my paper and paints on the dining room table and stared out the window hoping to catch a whiff of an idea of something to paint. A pair of wily animals caught my eye as they raced across the front yard chasing an obnoxious white cat named Fluffy. Part of me hoped they would catch the little snot, but the rest of me knew I had to go out and save her from a pair of coyotes looking for an easy meal.

Solow woke up and howled. Funny how he could always smell and hear right through my thick adobe walls. By the time he hopped on three legs to the door, I was on my way outside. I slammed the door hoping the coyotes would be startled by the sound. As I ran across the front yard and turned right at the corner of the house, I saw a white fluffy cat perched in my biggest oak tree and two coyotes running toward the top of the ridge a hundred yards behind the house.

Maybe I really should paint a picture of Fluffy. I liked the way the tree looked mysterious inside its giant green canopy, full of deep purple shadows, twisted grey limbs and pale patches wherever the sun put its mark. But the whitest, brightest thing around was that prissy cat wearing a Cheshire grin.

I ran in the kitchen door and grabbed my sketch pad and pencil. Solow wanted to follow me but I closed the door on him because I wanted Fluffy to hold her pose. Standing on the patio, I quickly sketched the scene and hurried back to my warm kitchen.

Amazingly, my painting developed the way I wanted it to—a pretty scene with an emphasis on gnarly limbs, interesting shadows, a cat sitting on a branch and two coyotes streaking up the hill in the distance. Fluffy's smug look told the rest of the story. I smiled and thanked God for my third painting.

A car door slammed outside.

Solow howled.

I checked the clock. It was almost six-thirty. Where did the time go? I pushed my hair back and opened the front door.

"Josie, honey, what's that green smear on your face?" David laughed.

"Come in and I'll show you." I walked him over to the dining room table where "Fluffy in a Tree" was air-drying.

"Hey, that's a great picture of my cat. Are those coyotes?" he asked, pointing to the two skinny creatures bounding up the hill.

"Yep, they chased her up a tree and she was nice enough to pose for me."

He kissed my cheek and walked me out to his Jeep, saying he had something to show me. I flipped on the porch light and immediately saw a large squarish thing tied to the top of his Jeep. He began untying the ropes, so I did my share of untying.

"Is that a mattress?" I asked.

"Yep, I want you to get a good night's sleep, no more complaining."

"When did I complain…."

"Let's see, there was…."

"Never mind. Maybe I brought it up a few times."

We kissed under the porch light, and our date began.

Chapter 8

Saturday morning I woke up rested and comfy on my new mattress. It was the sweetest early Christmas present in the whole world, but it meant I was back to only two paintings for the show. I would definitely frame "Fluffy in a Tree" and give it to David for Christmas. He loved the painting and he deserved more than the barbecue tongs I had planned to give him.

Not wanting to leave my warm bed, I closed my eyes and reviewed Friday evening with the Quintanas. It had been fun right up until Alicia happened to mention Mary's murder. When I told her I'd found a phone at the beach and had taken it to Jake to see if he could recover any pictures, David had rolled his eyes and said, "Not again."

I explained I was just helping Marla find closure.

Alicia had rolled her eyes on that one and Ernie cleared his throat and left the room, not wishing to get involved.

After dinner, Alicia and I took care of the dishes and cleaned the kitchen while the guys made frames in Ernie's workshop. We caught up to them later. Ernie and David sat on wooden stools discussing the Golden State Warriors' last game while Trigger, with great concentration, positioned pieces of wood in the miter box and sawed them. A stack of cut pieces waited to be glued and nailed. Two frames were finished except for stain, lacquer and a piece of glass.

"Anyone interested in dessert?" Alicia asked.

Trigger instantly put down the saw and led the way into the house, never shy about his mother's pecan pie. When we were finally up to our ears in pie and ice cream, David and I headed back to Aromas.

Remembering the very special evening was fun, but I needed to get up and start my day. I pushed the blankets back and climbed out of bed. Solow's bed was empty. I found him waiting patiently at the back door and let him out. I didn't think a three-legged basset would be able to run fast, but Solow saw Fluffy and put everything he had into the chase, including the leg in a brace. A minute later, I heard a yelp and a long mournful howl, not Solow's typical howl.

Dressed in pajamas and bare feet, I sprinted to the back of the house, turned the corner and saw Solow near the far end of the back of the house. I plodded over to him, cold mud squishing between my toes, flannel pant legs dragging. Poor Solow had three out of four legs stuck in sucky squishy mud. I wrapped my arms around his belly and with great effort pulled him a couple feet over to higher ground.

A small white thing half covered in mud caught my eye. A closer look showed it to be a medicine bottle. My first thought was, what a funny place to find a medicine bottle, or anything for that matter since the only thing in my back yard was a tin storage shed and a bazillion weeds that David had kindly mowed for me.

I couldn't get any dirtier than I already was, so I stepped back into the mud and picked up the medicine bottle. An electric shock zipped through my body when I read Mary Milford's name on the label. But it only took a second to realize the connection between Mel falling off the roof and finding his sister's medicine.

Solow tucked his tail between his legs and followed me back to the patio. I held his collar with my left hand and the hose with my right. He shook cold water all over me, but it didn't matter because I was already cold, muddy and ready for a nice warm shower. But standing under warm water felt like I was being pelted with hot prickly spears at first. Gradually the shower began to feel good, too good. Like my new mattress, I didn't want to leave it, but duty called—just fourteen days left to create a great collection of artwork. I turned off the water and toweled myself dry.

The phone rang.

I dashed to the kitchen wrapped in a white towel. "Hello?" My wet hair dripped water. I shivered.

"G'day, Josephine, this is Jake…."

My heart stopped beating for a second. I took a deep breath and asked if he'd been able to recover anything from the phone.

Jake said he hadn't had time yet, but said he had a question for me. Did anyone else know about the phone and should he share information about the phone if someone asked about it….?

"Jake, who asked about the phone? Do you have a name?"

"It's this ol' bloke I never saw before, said his name is Kirby Levitt, claims he's a well-known surfer around these parts."

"Oh my God, Mary's boyfriend's name is Kirby. Don't you dare share anything with him, and call me as soon as you find pictures on the phone. I really appreciate you calling me about this Kirby guy." We hung up.

Still wrapped in a towel, I grabbed the phone book and looked up Mr. Levitt. According to the phonebook he lived on Emerald Street. I remembered seeing the street in the jewel district of Capitola, just a few blocks from Marla's house. I picked up the phone and punched in Marla's number.

"Hello."

"Hi, Marla, glad I caught you at home. It seems that a friend of mine knows a friend of yours, Kirby Levitt."

"Why yes, he's a friend of the family. Mary and I went to school with Kirby. Our families have always been close. Is there some sort of problem, Josephine? Is Kirby all right?"

"This friend of mine lost Kirby's phone number, that's all. Do you have his work phone?"

"Well, yes. He still works for the *Sentinel.* Your friend should know that."

"To tell you the truth, I was…I mean my friend was just wondering what Kirby is like, you know, does he have a temper, hold grudges—that sort of thing…?"

"Josephine, what are you getting at? Kirby is our friend."

"It's nothing important. Sorry to bother you, Marla." I hung up quickly, completely embarrassed. There had to be a better way of getting information. Standing in the kitchen in a puddle of water, red-faced and discouraged, I put Mr. Coffee to work. At least I'd have the comfort of a hot cup of my favorite brew to go along with a beautiful bacon and cheese omelet.

An hour later, I was dressed in my favorite jeans and yellow blouse in case David came over to see me. I pulled on a warm jacket and took a short walk to the mailbox at the end of my driveway. Solow trotted along on three legs. I raked a stack of mostly unwanted mailer gimmicks into my arms, shut the mailbox and called Solow. He hopped along at my side up to the front door.

As we entered the living room, an engine roared, gravel crunched and Solow barked. I parted the dining room drapes and looked out the window at a middle-aged man getting out of a blue Porsche parked behind my truck. The pot-bellied sixty-five-year-old gentleman, wearing a navy blue hoodie and low-riding jeans, sauntered up to the front door with attitude.

Solow's barks sharpened.

"Who's there?" I asked through the door.

Solow growled.

"My name is Kirby....Marla's friend."

I opened the door.

"I need to talk to you about a mutual friend," he smiled.

I let the man in, wondering how Kirby knew where I lived until I remembered my last conversation with Marla.

"Like I said, my name is Kirby Levitt...your eyes are so green," he cooed. "A bit of the Irish?"

"Ah, yeah, a little bit on Dad's side." What did this old codger-teenage-wanna-be want with me? I pealed off my jacket and offered Kirby a seat on the couch. His eyes were glued to my yellow shirt and his smile never wavered.

Feeling unnerved, I excused myself, hurried down the hall to my room and slipped on a roomy button down denim shirt over the yellow blouse. I checked the mirror. Yep, it covered my voluptuousness pretty well. When I returned to the living room, Kirby had charmed Solow with his syrupy voice and ear rubs.

"That was quick. I liked the first outfit the best," he grinned.

You dirty old man, I thought to myself. "Would you care for a cup of coffee?"

"Hey, that would be cool." He pushed his hood back and down, exposing a handful of brittle-looking bronze colored hair. He had a winter tan and his thick dark eyebrows gave him a Groucho Marks look. Dark brown eyes roamed all over me and the kitchen. Reaching for the coffee cups, I felt his stare, but the worst part was when I turned around. Something green was caught in the little space between his two front abnormally white teeth, as he smiled and smiled and smiled. Was this guy for real?

I poured two cups of coffee and we sat down at the kitchen table.

"I hear you write for the *Sentinel*," I said and offered him cream and sugar.

"Yeah, that's right. I write about the Santa Cruz surfing scene—stuff like that. I do a little surfing myself when I have time." He winked, drank coffee, ogled me and bragged about himself all at the same time. Even Solow figured out the old braggart pretty fast and left the room.

"Kirby, did you know that Mary was taking pain pills?"

"No." He cocked his head. "Why do you think she needed pills?"

"I thought you would know. By the way, is that Mary's car you're driving?"

"It was Mary's but she willed it to me…not formally, but she told Marla it would go to me if anything happened to her."

"You still haven't told me why you're here…."

There were two quick knocks on the back door.

Solow ran through the kitchen barking and wagging his tail.

David walked into the room. He looked at me. He looked at Kirby and laughed. "You old son-of-a-gun!"

Kirby stood up and the men shook hands.

David explained to me that he and Kirby had a history going way back to the Santa Cruz Boardwalk when he was a teenager and Kirby had hired him to run the Ferris wheel. They worked together three summers in a row, until David went off to college. He said he still reads Kirby's column whenever he can.

Groucho exercised his impressive eyebrows as he filled David in on his life after the boardwalk. Summing it up, he spent three years in the service, came home to live with his mother, surfed and currently writes a surfing column for the *Santa Cruz Sentinel.* Big wow.

David's story was much more interesting, one divorce ten years ago, a long and distinguished career with IBM, early retirement and a wonderful relationship with me. I listened while he made that last point very clear.

"Good for you, old man," Kirby grinned. "She's a looker."

"So what are you doing in Aromas?" David asked.

"You mean in your girlfriend's house? We have some mutual friends. I think Josephine found out Mary was my girlfriend…."

"You mean your girlfriend was the same Mary who fell off the cliff?" David looked mortified.

"Yep, poor Mary, such a nice person."

Because of the snappy way Kirby said it I knew he never loved Mary. What was his reason for dating her all those years? He didn't look like he was in mourning, staring at me with goo-goo eyes for the nineteenth time. I poured a cup of coffee for David and topped off Kirby's, wishing I had the nerve to pour it down his shirt. I turned my head and smiled at the thought.

"I still don't know what you want to talk about, Kirby," I said, waiting to see if he'd mention Jake and the smashed up phone.

"I was talking to Marla recently and she said you stayed over night at her house and the next day she was looking for Mary's diary on account of I asked her for it. She couldn't find it anywhere…."

"You think I have it?" I said, feeling my face heating up.

"Well, I just thought maybe you saw it somewhere, that's all."

"What do you expect to find in the diary?" I asked.

"Not much, the usual stuff." Kirby turned his attention to Solow who was sniffing his pant leg. "Nice dog you got here."

Thankfully the journal subject was forgotten and the smashed phone subject never came up. David invited Kirby to walk next door to see his newest project, a gazebo he was building between his pond and an extensive brick barbecue and pizza oven structure.

The minute the guys left, I began a new painting. This time I painted the Capitola cliffs from memory, not from the top looking down into a stormy sea, but from the beach looking up. I remembered the high craggy cliff with its interesting features and shadows, not to mention the wooden stairs. I added the two little boys playing while their mom lay on a beach towel with a book over her face. I sprinkled salt on the wet sand color. When the paint was dry I blew the salt away. Suddenly the sand in the foreground had texture.

I decided the painting was a keeper, so I placed it in a large cardboard portfolio with the other three finished pieces. Thirteen paint days left. Alicia mentioned she was starting her tenth painting, but I didn't care. It wasn't a contest. I just wanted to sell a couple of paintings to recoup my half of the booth fee. But even more than that, I wanted to see if my paintings were salable, would people like them. Sometimes an artist needs to know she's appreciated.

Chapter 9

Mom called Sunday morning to remind me about Sunday dinner. Heaven knows I ate at my parent's house fifty times more often than they ate at my house. The exception to that fact was the annual Christmas party at my house. The Quintanas would be coming, plus David and his son and granddaughter, Robert and possibly Robert's niece and nephew. Mom and Dad would bring their neighbor, Myrtle. I had two and a half weeks to get a tree up and decorated, plan the menu and shop for food. But first I needed to paint.

The sun came out about noon, giving me a perfect opportunity to paint outside. I hauled my gear to the west side of the house and sketched the green hills dotted with oaks. It was a simple and serene scene, pleasing to the eye. I finished the grassy hills and was just about to add the oaks when David strolled up to me.

"Are we still going to cut down a Christmas tree?"

"Sorry, I forgot. I'll finish this some other time."

David helped me carry everything into the house.

"Which tree farm do you want to go to?" I asked.

"The one with the sheep is the closest…."

"Sounds good," I said, looking forward to roaming the hills on a nice sunny day. As usual, we would cut down a lovely Monterey Pine and set it up in my living room. David never wanted his own tree. He liked having an excuse to come over and enjoy mine.

We found a full-figured pine with all its boughs in the right places. I made the first cut into the base of the tree which I'd already named Myrtle for her unabashed shapeliness. Expecting David's usual offer to finish the sawing, I raised up and looked around, finally spotting him a couple acres away at the top of a knoll. Cutting a tree! Many thoughts ran through my head like, "Why didn't he tell me he wanted a tree?" and, "Be still, Josephine, you're not his mother."

Automatically, I saw it as a race. Who would saw their tree down first? I gave it everything I had. Sweat dripped down my forehead. I gave my little saw the last heave-ho. Myrtle hit the ground with a soft woosh. I looked up as David walked up to me and introduced his tree named Bob, a perky pine big enough to tickle a fourteen-foot ceiling. Too bad his ceiling was only ten-foot.

"I know it's big," he said. "I'll just trim it when I get home."

I turned away so he wouldn't see me roll my eyes. "Who's that over there? Is that Robert…and look, there's his niece and nephew. Those trees aren't for climbing…there goes Robert, chasing them away."

"Poor guy has his hands full with the monsters. Did I tell you that Harley and Monica will be staying with me for a couple days at Christmas time and going to your house on Christmas Day?"

"Is that why you need a tree?"

"Yep…look at those kids run. Robert doesn't stand a chance," he laughed.

"I'm glad Harley and Monica are coming," I said. I had a great relationship with David's son and five-year-old granddaughter.

David and I hauled our trees down to the three-sided shingled shack where a guy in a Santa hat ushered us into a line of people adopting trees. He offered us a cup of hot cider. We sipped cider and waited for six trees ahead of us to be measured and wrapped with twine.

Robert stood in line behind us, head cranking left and right, eyes rapidly searching the grounds for two over-active half-grown kids.

"Nothing like a family outing," I said to Robert.

"Yeah, my sister's laid up with a hernia…."

"That's too bad. I talked to your friend, Jake."

"Did I tell you what a great surfer he is?"

"No, but he sure looked happy to have the project I gave him."

"How's your painting coming along?" Robert asked.

"Painted half a picture today. Now I have almost four for the sale."

"I know of a guy with cheap frames."

"Inexpensive or cheap?" I asked.

"I have no use for frames but Mom thought they were very inexpensive. This guy they call Buzz sells them out of his garage."

"I think I know Buzz. I'll give him a call." I figured chances where good Robert was talking about old Mr. Buzznick and I had the man's phone number on the watercolor class phone list at home.

I hoisted Myrtle into the back of David's Jeep. She filled the interior, back to front. Her pointy tip rested on the dash, a rogue branch tickled my neck.

David tied Bob to the roof using half-a-dozen bungee cords. The big pine over-extended his Jeep, front and back, its top flopping against the middle of the windshield as we cautiously cruised two miles back to Otis.

David hauled my tree onto the front porch and leaned it against the wall. He gave me a peck on the cheek and said he'd be back in a little while to take me to dinner at Mom and Dad's.

I hurried over to the tin shed behind the house and grabbed the first bucket I saw, being careful not to touch spider webs. I filled the bucket with water, and lowered Myrtle's sappy trunk into the water. I would deal with putting her into the tree stand when I had more time. It was a job David had performed for the last ten years, but I wasn't helpless. I would do it myself.

Glancing at the wall clock in the kitchen, I realized I still had an hour an a half to finish my painting and then jump into some clean clothes for our dinner at Mom and Dad's.

I quickly lugged my paint box and half-finished painting out to the back of my property at the base of the hill. The afternoon was quiet as grass, dry and comfortable. Solow lay by my side as I sat on my paint box, paper and board on my lap. After painting several oak trees and adding wild flowers taken from my imagination, the painting was almost finished.

Suddenly Solow raised his head and howled.

I looked up from my work in time to see a coyote streaking across the hillside with something furry white in his mouth, followed by another coyote. This was the second time coyotes had crossed my property in daylight. I thought about the first time.

"Oh no!" I dropped the board and stood up. "They got Fluffy!"

Solow jumped into action. Unfortunately, my painting was in his way. I watched in slow motion as his toenails churned across the wet paper, looking for traction. At basset speed, he hopped across the grassy field on three legs, bellowing his frustration as he tried his best to catch up to the wily coyotes.

I didn't know that I held any good feelings for Fluffy, but the lump in my throat said that I did. There was no way to save her. I imagined David's heat-broken face. The coyotes had already disappeared over the ridge into a maze of eucalyptus. All that was left was to report the bad news to my dear friend.

A tear ran down my cheek. I wiped it away as we crossed the field. I wondered if Solow felt sad, after all, he had spent more time with Fluffy than any other creature except David. He caught up to me just as the back of David's house came into view.

The lump in my throat got bigger. Poor David.

Solow stayed with me as we walked across David's patio and I peeked through the window in the back door of his garage. The door was locked. He didn't hear me knocking because he was busy giving Bob a haircut with the hedge trimmer. Bob looked like a ten-foot guy just back from the near-sighted, shaky-handed worst barber in town.

We rounded the garage and entered through the big open double door.

David saw us and cut the motor.

"Oh, David...." My voice squeaked, then quit on me.

"What's the matter, honey?" He set the trimmer on the floor and put his arm around me. "I know Bob isn't perfect, but...."

"No, not Bob...sniff...Fluf–fy."

"What about Fluffy? She's in the house. She doesn't like the sound of the trimmer."

"Are you sure?" I stepped over to the kitchen door and opened it. My first glance into the house from the garage told me how wrong I had been. I saw Fluffy's tail swishing back and forth as she relaxed on a chair pushed up to the kitchen table. The lump in my throat dissolved, the tears dried up and some bad thoughts ran through my mind. I ignored them and told David how happy I was to see his cat. I didn't even mention my ruined painting.

David checked his watch. "I think we better get into some clean clothes. Your folks won't like it if we're late."

I turned to go.

"Wait a minute; why were you so worried about Fluffy?"

"I thought the coyotes got her. Apparently they got a rabbit or something." I shuffled off to my house, but Solow stayed with David, all the better to see how Bob would turn out—which proved my theory about men and machines.

I dumped the shredded painting in the garbage, gathered up my painting equipment and dropped it all on the dinning room table.

The phone rang.

"Hello"

"Hello, dear. Leola wants you to bring cinnamon. She's making banana bread and ran out."

"Okay, Dad, see you in about an hour." We hung up. I found a bottle of cinnamon and dropped it into my purse. After a fast shower I dressed myself in black cords, a green button-down blouse and a black cardigan. I slipped my feet into a pair of black boots, hooked jade earrings into my pierced ears, powdered my nose and carefully covered my lips with tangerine lipstick.

I heard knocking on the front door and a howl from Solow. I let the boys in, quickly fed Solow his dinner and took off for Santa Cruz with David. The sun had set and the stars were out as we entered Highway One north heading for Santa Cruz, population 64,000, situated 35 minutes and ten worlds away from the southern end of the county where David and I lived. But it was always fun to see what the natives were up to—the natives being the street people, performers and college students.

As we cruised Pacific Avenue in down town Santa Cruz, we talked about the festive decorations along the main street, including some highly decorated young adults. Several music groups had set up their equipment on the sidewalks. City sandwich boards warned of a "holiday" parade at eight p.m. It was only six-thirty and the place was jammed with traffic, pedestrians and police units.

David left Pacific Avenue, turned onto Walnut, and parked at the curb in front of a 1940's bungalow I had called "home" for the first twenty years of my life. Growing up in Santa Cruz had been every child's dream, plenty of beach time, hiking, biking, roller skating and trips to the redwood forest. Mom and Dad were typical Santa Cruz citizens, still hiking, biking, skating, kayaking, bowling and making the most of their senior years.

Mom greeted us at the door wearing her red sari and gold sandals. Her outfit contrasted nicely with the lush green Christmas tree in the corner. Piney fragrance and fifty-year-old ornaments swept me back to my childhood. It was the same old house, a similar tree and Bing Crosby singing *White Christmas*. A CD replaced the old phonograph, but the warm happy feeling was the same.

Dad walked into the room wearing dark cords and a green vest over his red and green plaid shirt. He and David shook hands. I got the big hug.

"Did you bring cinnamon for your mother?" he asked.

I pulled the bottle out of my purse and handed it to Mom. She had one dessert she could count on—banana bread. Cooking was never her forte. Her real talent was speaking to her rose club, book club, dinner club and racket club, and raising money for charity. Dad was more comfortable with his bowling team, but both of them stayed active even though they were only two candles shy of eighty.

"Bob, put another log on the fire, would you, dear?" Mom said as she pulled me into the kitchen. She busied herself stirring cinnamon into the bread dough while I answered the tapping on the back door. Myrtle fluttered into the kitchen carrying a bottle of wine and a sack of dinner rolls, her yearly contribution to Christmas dinner. On Christmas Day, Myrtle would deliver the same thing to my house because she had given up cooking years ago.

"I heard David say that you two cut Christmas trees today…." Mom said.

"Yeah, this year he wanted one in his house because Harley and Monica are coming for a visit. Do you have a tree, Myrtle?"

"I'm not looking for projects, dear. That's why I come here to visit and enjoy the Christmas decorations," she smiled. Her black curly wig leaned left a notch as she pulled her round little body onto a stool at the breakfast bar. Opaque nylons folded around her ankles when she crossed her chubby legs. She had spiced up her yellow pantsuit with a long black and yellow patterned scarf, her signature outfit for the last ten years.

The bread baked, the roast rested and the three of us caught up on gossip because Myrtle knew everything about everyone. Coincidentally, Mary Milford was the daughter of one of her old school-mates. Myrtle also knew Marla and Mel. She commented on Mel's nasty divorce.

"Myrtle, did you know that Mary Milford fell off a cliff in Capitola?" I asked.

"Yes, poor dear. She really wasn't herself after that terrible car crash. They say she'd been drinking, but I wouldn't say anything about that. It happened way out on Branciforte Drive. She was visiting her friend who lives in a nice home up there in the forest…so it's evening and dark when she pulls onto the road and t-bones this car with a mom, dad and little girl in it. Mary claimed the car didn't have its lights on."

"Do you think that was true?" I asked.

"Of course it wasn't true." Mom said.

"We'll never know because the people spoke very little English, their car was old and they didn't want to call the Highway Patrol," Myrtle added. "For sure, they didn't have insurance. Mary didn't want to call the police either because she'd had a bit of wine with her dinner, so she literally stuffs the mom, dad and little girl into her dented up Porsche and takes them to her house in Capitola. My best friend got all this from Mary's best friend."

I rolled my eyes. "I can't believe they didn't call 911. I heard that the driver was crippled in that accident."

"You're right about that." Myrtle rolled her eyes and shook her head slowly. "Being new in this country, the man was too scared to go to the hospital, so Mary bought him a wheel chair. In fact, she had the family living with her and Marla last I heard."

"Sounds to me like Mary suffered from too much guilt," Leola said.

"I think you're right, Mom. Marla told me that Mary had rooms built in her garage for the family and she bought groceries for them and everything."

Myrtle twisted around in her seat. "Leola, is that smoke coming from the oven?"

"Oh dear, the banana bread!"

Chapter 10

Monday morning I woke up thinking about twelve more days before the Christmas Art Festival, twelve more chances to create paintings for the show. After breakfast I called Buzz. He asked for a message. I left one. An hour later he called back.

"Hi, Josephine, what can I do for you?"

"Hi, Buzz. As you know, Alicia and I will be selling our paintings at the grange Christmas sale and I heard that you have frames for sale."

"What size and how many?"

"I'm hoping to have at least nine or ten paintings. Actually, I have four so far, but one of them is for my boyfriend. I've been working at it really hard but I ran into a little bad luck…."

"Yeah, well, can you tell me the sizes?"

"They're all the same size—twelve by seventeen—but when they're matted they'll be fourteen by eighteen inches."

"Good, a very popular size. I have a whole bunch. With glass?" he asked.

"Yep, with glass. I should probably come over and see them…."

"I live in Soquel, over on Victory Lane. My house is the first one on the left, the one with the flag pole on the lawn. You can't miss it." Buzz suggested I come over to his place before noon because he had a lunch appointment. It sounded like he might be meeting up with a lady friend. I detected a bit of *oo-la-la* in his voice.

I finished cleaning the kitchen and piled Solow into the truck for a ride to Soquel (Sew-kell), a small town located just east of Capitola. The day was cool but sunny with big puffy clouds coming in from the north. Solow whipped his tail side to side as he watched the scenery streaming by. The moment we turned onto Victory Lane, I knew we were looking at Buzz' house. The first house on the left had a commercial-size flag pole with a large American flag at the top and a smaller green flag featuring a rabbit wearing a Santa hat below the big flag.

My right front tire bounced over a curb and Solow's head hit the roof as I stared at the weird bunny.

I pulled in beside Buzz' Mustang and cut the engine. The garage door opened and Buzz welcomed us into his shop. The garage was filled with tables displaying various craft items. One long table displayed a dozen different sizes and types of frames. Buzz pointed to the cardboard boxes under the table.

"Pick out what you want and I'll find it in these here boxes."

"Do you mind if Solow wanders around?"

"Heck no, I love animals....what the....he peed on my box of soap stone."

"Sorry, Buzz." I quickly grabbed Solow's collar and hauled him back into the truck.

"It's okay, I love animals." But his red face didn't look happy.

"Nice bunny flag up there...."

"Oh, that; I figure it covers Christmas and Easter pretty well. Good for business."

I explained that I only wanted six frames. He looked a little disappointed. I told him I'd come back next week for the rest, assuming I had more paintings by then. He found the box containing the fourteen by eighteen inch frames and pulled out six plastic bags, each containing four cut pieces of wood and a packet of hardware. The sheets of glass came from another box.

Buzz had stacks of empty boxes along one wall. He chose one and carefully placed my framing material inside with newspaper to cushion the glass. When he finished, he looked at me with his good eye. I guess I looked worried.

"Josephine, would you like me to put the frames together for you for a small charge?"

My shoulders relaxed. "Would you, please?" I felt my shoulders relax.

"I'll put ten of them together in case you need a few more. I sell a lot in this size. You'll need mats too. Buzz' chest swelled as he demonstrated his thoughtful and successful *persona gratae*.

"Buzz, how long have you known Kirby?"

"Kirby? We go way back. He dated Mary for years, until she lost interest in his selfish, braggin,' surfin' old body."

"Okay, thanks, Buzz. I'll see you Friday." I jumped into my truck and took off for Marla's house in Capitola, wondering about Buzz' real connection with Kirby and Mary. If Buzz was an honest man he would have mentioned the fact that he, and Vick and Kirby had joined the service together many years ago, unless Vick wasn't telling the truth.

Solow opened one bloodshot eye and flapped his tail on the seat.

"We're at Marla's house now. You be a good boy while I look around." I rolled his window down to half-mast, climbed out of my seat and slammed the door. Marla's SUV was missing, but I walked up to the front door anyway and rang the bell. I thought about looking under the door mat for the key, but noticed my umbrella leaning against a potted geranium at the other end of the front porch. She obviously had left it there for me. Why did she have to be so thoughtful?

Not wanting to waste a trip to Capitola, I walked across the lawn, turned left at the garden gate and took a narrow path to Marla's back yard. I walked up to the garage side door and knocked. No one came to the door so I opened it and moved on down to Mel's door. He heard my knocking and answered the door, still wearing a brace, a boot and a five o'clock shadow.

"Josephine?" He straightened his t-shirt.

"Hi, Mel, I just came by to see how you're doing. Are you healing pretty well?"

"Yeah, but I just got turned down for disability," he grumped.

"That's too bad, but you don't have to pay rent…."

"I pay rent, *they* don't." He pointed to the wall separating his room from the Herrera's. Through the wall came the sound of hammering.

"What is that noise?" I asked.

"I really don't know. It sounds like hammering nails into wood, but the guy's in a wheel chair and his wife is working in a convalescent hospital down the street. I don't think the little girl would be hammering."

"What's Mr. Herrera like?"

"I don't know. Marla told me he used to be a carpenter. I only saw him once…I needed to talk to the mom. She answered the door and he was sitting in his wheelchair behind her with a blanket over his legs. The little girl did most of the talking."

"I talked to my insurance guy and it looks like you'll be reimbursed for the hospital bill and maybe a few dollars for missed work."

"That's good news," he smiled.

"But it'll be awhile—red tape and all." I looked at my watch. "Oh, look at the time!" I excused myself and hurried back to my truck. It was noon and I had a date with a paint brush. Painting ideas floated across my mind all the way home—some good, some ugly and some really stupid.

I parked in front of my house and immediately noticed Myrtle lying on her side. Her sticky trunk oozed sap and sucked air from an empty bucket like a guppy out of water. She looked anemic. The poor girl needed a proper tree holder, but I needed to paint first. Since the hose was still in the muddy back yard, I went inside and filled a large cooking pot with water.

The phone rang. I put the pot down on the counter and answered the phone. It was Mom calling to tell me I'd left my sweater at her house. I hadn't even missed it.

My stomach growled, making my next priority a lovely bagel with liverwurst, creamed cheese and a fat slice of tomato. Solow hopped into the kitchen, hoping to share my lunch. When I was finished eating, I gave him the one piece I had saved. He swallowed it whole, and laid down for another nap.

I threw a load of wash in the washing machine and taped a fresh piece of watercolor paper to my board. The phone rang. It was Alicia.

"Jo, where have you been? You don't answer your cell or the house phone…"

"I just answered the house phone. By the way, I found a great price on frames. Buzz is selling them out of his garage."

"That's nice to know. Trigger's having a hard time keeping up with my paintings."

"Me too, in fact, I was just about to start painting when you called."

"Why did you answer the phone? You could have listened to a message instead." Alicia laughed.

"You know me pretty well. I answered it because I don't have a clue about what to paint. Please give me an idea," I begged.

"Sorry, Jo, gotta run."

We hung up.

Earlier I had considered painting the view from my dining room table, green grass—better known as weeds, wild lilacs in bloom, and oak and redwood in the distance. Even though it was winter and the sky was grey, I began laying in a blue sky with a few wispy clouds. I worked so hard I forgot about everything else. When I finally finished the painting, straightened my back and checking the clock, it was almost five and getting dark outside.

I decided to take Solow for a walk down to the mailbox before it was too dark to see. On the way back, I saw Myrtle lying on the porch gasping for water. My heart went out to her, but the phone was ringing so I dashed inside to answer it.

"Hi, Josephine; its Vick here."

"Hi, Vick; what's going on?"

"After having breakfast with you and Claudia the other day, I realized how serious you are about finding Mary's murderer. I don't usually rat on my friends, but I have something to tell you. Mind if I come over…?"

"Of course I don't mind, but I'll meet you half-way in Watsonville…ah, because I need to go to the grocery store. Can you meet me at the store on Eastlake at seven? I'm driving an older model red Mazda pickup."

"Yeah, that'll work for me. See you in a couple hours."

After a quick meal for myself and Solow, we climbed into the truck and I drove to the Watsonville grocery store. I parked under one of a dozen security lights and cracked a window open for Solow, even though it was a cool fifty degrees outside. By my watch, I had twenty minutes to shop before Vick was scheduled to roll into the neighborhood.

I walked past a white SUV that looked a lot like Marla's; even the "Save the Cows, eat Tuna," bumper sticker looked familiar. Sure enough, I bumped into her on aisle five. As I turned a corner, our baskets smacked together.

"Oh, Josephine, so sorry," she said, pulling her cart back from mine.

"It was my fault, Marla." I tossed a sack of kibble into my cart.

Marla said, "Did you know that the chickens and turkeys they use in that kibble eat slop? I heard it from my neighbor. She used to work at the plant where they make the stuff, back there in Massachusetts."

"Well, I don't have a choice; it's the only one Solow likes. Are you on your way home from work?"

"Yes, long day today," she sighed.

"I picked up my umbrella. Thanks for putting it on the porch." I pushed my cart around the corner before she could say any more. I wanted to ask her if she would give Mel a break on the rent now that he couldn't work, but it wasn't my business. Instead, I loaded my cart with groceries and rolled it up to Robert's check stand.

"Robert, you're working late."

"I volunteered to fill in—better than babysitting. Have you heard anything from old Leadfoot?"

"No, not yet. Are the cantaloupes any good?"

"Glad you asked. They're tasteless," he said, setting the melon I had picked out aside. "But these berries are excellent." Robert totaled the lot and bagged everything. He would have carried the bags out to the truck for me, but Marla pushed her cart into his line at the last minute.

"See ya, Robert, Marla." I pushed the cart out to my truck. An older red Miata convertible cooled its wheels in the space next to mine. Icky cologne wafted my way even before Vick climbed out of the car and helped me load the groceries into the back of my truck.

We stood under the yellow lamplight, shivering as the wind picked up and the temperature dipped. I zipped my jacket and raised the collar.

Vick wore a leather bomber jacket, tight jeans and pointy toed boots.

"You have some information for me, Vick?"

Mr. 'Deep Throat' stepped closer. "You're probably looking for a motive—after all, Mary was a very nice lady. But the truth is she didn't treat Kirby very well. She should have just married the poor guy instead of leading him on for the last forty years."

"That's funny; the story I heard was that Kirby wouldn't commit." I shivered. "Are you saying that Kirby had something to do with her death?"

"Heck no; he's my friend. I just thought I should tell you what was really going on. I feel it's my duty, besides, Kirby has a temper. And who do you think inherited Mary's Porsche?"

"Kirby."

"Right, but Buzz inherited her stock in IBM."

My jaw dropped. "So Buzz was buzzing around the honey too?"

"Seems that way. I left her alone," Vick declared, as he climbed back into his little Miata and slammed the door.

Another door slammed nearby. A white SUV quietly rolled out of the dimly lit parking lot.

I fired up the engine and cruised home, my mind processing Vick's words. It finally hit me, the only way to find out if the insinuations were true was to read Mary's diary. I yawned. It would be a long night.

Chapter 11

A new day dawned. Tuesday was a new chance to create art, and hopefully I'd add another painting to my puny art festival collection—if only I could stay awake long enough to complete one whole painting. I had fallen asleep at two in the morning in my chair. Five hours later, I woke up as light poured through the living room windows. Mary's five-year journal lay on the floor. I remembered reading her last year—up to the entries for the month of November.

Solow woke up and ran to the kitchen to check his bowl. One minute later he was back at my side, bloodshot eyes following my every move, especially the trip to the back door. I let him out and turned to Mr. Coffee. A calendar hung on the wall behind Mr. Coffee. The picture for December was a warm cozy scene of Santa asleep in his chair, a fire in the fireplace and a big yellow dog at his feet. I decided that was the picture I would paint.

As I prepared breakfast for Solow and myself, I thought about substituting Solow for the big yellow dog in the calendar picture. As it turned out, I made several substitutions. My painting didn't look very much like the original, but I felt it was a keeper. Even if it didn't look good, I would have kept it since it took all day to complete. I had a lot of time and effort invested in the painting. Besides, the Solow part of the picture looked adorable with his long ears splayed on the braided rug.

At four in the afternoon, my eyelids were heavy. I reheated old coffee and picked up the journal. Mid-

November, Mary wrote that she told Buzz to buzz-off. After years of juggling dates with Buzz and Kirby, she finally was tired of Buzz and told him so. Was that the silver bullet? I thought it might be, until I read an entry for a week later when she told Kirby to take a hike and made up with Buzz.

I scratched my head, feeling totally confused.

Solow woke up and howled.

It was getting dark outside so I flipped the porch light on and peeked out the window.

Marla climbed out of her white Lexus.

Solow's barks became urgent.

I held him back and stepped outside. "Hi, Marla…."

"Josephine, we need to talk," she snapped, red-faced, as she thrust the front door open.

I followed her inside.

Solow stepped quietly out of her way.

The first thing she saw was Mary's open diary on the coffee table where I'd left it. Her whole body quivered with rage as she grabbed the book and pushed it into her purse.

I stepped back. "I'm investigating…."

"Investigating, my foot! You leave me and my family alone, you, you big snoop!" She stamped her foot. "Do you understand?"

"What did you want to talk about…?"

Without answering, she stormed out of the house, climbed into her vehicle and fish-tailed down the driveway.

It would have been easy for me to shrug off the insults and forget the whole incident, but some of what she said was true. I couldn't forget her wild-eyed look when she saw the book, and her shaking hands as she pulled the front door open for a quick exit.

For my own sanity I had to know that Marla made it home safely.

I pushed the accelerator hard as my truck sped down Otis onto San Juan Road. I figured I was just a few minutes behind her. My high beams rapidly ate up the dark empty road ahead. I thought about Marla being fired because of too many traffic tickets and drove even faster.

"Oh no!" I yelled at the train moving slowly down the tracks. It felt like an eternity before the rear engine of the train finally disappeared into the night and the safety arms lifted into their up-position. My Mazda shot across the tracks and roared down the dark empty road. Where was Marla? If she'd taken Highway 129 instead of San Juan, I would never find her. I drove several miles without seeing a single car coming or going. Apparently most commuters were already home from work, enjoying their families.

Even though I drove at twice the speed limit, a set of red and blue flashing lights caught up to me and flew by my truck like a greyhound passing a tricycle. A minute later, I saw the flashing lights again. I pulled up behind the Highway Patrol car, cut the engine and ran on foot past a yellow pickup and into a lettuce field where the patrol car's spotlight had glommed onto Marla's SUV. It was clear that she'd flipped her vehicle over the drainage ditch and slid up-side-down a good thirty feet across an unsuspecting lettuce field. A pile of clipped heads of lettuce covered the windshield. Four tires spun slowly under a moonless sky.

"Lady, what are you doing out here?"

"Sorry, Officer, I think my friend might be in that car."

He quickly forgot about me as he talked into his radio, calling for more help. I trudged through rows of lettuce and mud until I was close enough to read an upside down bumper sticker, "Save a Cow, eat Tuna."

My hunch was right. Marla did crash her car, but where was she?

"Marla?" I heard a whimper and looked up. "Oh my…you're upside down!"

The officer walked up to the car door and tried to open it.

"Ma'am, can you reach the door lock?"

"Help me!" she cried.

"Give it another try, ma'am. You can do it," he encouraged her between phone calls.

"Come on, Marla, you can do it…just stretch your arm a little more." What if she quit trying, just to spite me. But she tried again. The trunk popped open, the flap over the gas tank opened and then we heard the click-sound we were waiting for. The officer pulled the door open and put his arms up around Marla's torso.

"I gotcha; now unbuckle your seatbelt."

Marla's eyes looked big and scared. "You better catch me!" she said just before she clicked the belt free. The officer's knees buckled and they both landed in the mud. Something fell out of the front seat.

Sirens grew louder, then silence. More sirens, more flashing red lights. Three firemen ran into the muddy field carrying a stretcher and medical equipment. They plugged an IV into Marla's arm and handed her off to the ambulance guys who'd just arrived.

No one paid attention to me standing in the dark. As soon as the rescuers carried Marla to the roadside, I walked closer to her car, casually leaned down and picked up the fallen item. I tucked the muddy thing under my jacket, turned and headed back to my truck.

Two county sheriff's cars were parked on the other side of the road. A tow truck pulled in behind my truck as I slogged my way across the ditch.

"Hey, lady, is that your pickup?" a sheriff's deputy yelled.

"Yep, I'm leaving right now." I started the engine, still watching the first responders as they loaded Marla into an ambulance. The siren blared. I followed the well-lit vehicle west on San Juan Road at a moderate speed because my legs felt shaky and weak and my heart thumped sporadically in my chest.

By the time I arrived at Watsonville hospital, Marla had already been rolled into the emergency room. I parked, put the interior light on and examined Mary's journal. I used Kleenex and hand sanitizer from my purse to wipe the effected parts of the cover and pages clean. Not totally clean, but passable.

I planned to visit Marla as soon as her condition stabilized—whatever that condition was. In the meantime, I did some light reading from the only book around, concentrating on Mary's October and November entries.

October 27

I'm worried about Pedro taking too many pills. I will give him half as many next time. Laurita brought home a kitten today. I hope she is allowed to keep it as she has so little.

October 28

I told Pedro my plan to wean him off the meds. He didn't say anything. I can tell he is upset. Laurita was allowed to keep the kitten. I'm so happy.

October 29

I picked up my prescription this morning. Doc wants to do some tests. Hope he won't stop my pills. Juanita got a promotion—very happy for her. Went to a movie with Buzz—same old problem, I give up.

October 30

Kirby called—said he called last night. Where was I? He came looking for me and spent the evening with Marla. She says he's a braggart and a blow-hard. I can't argue with that. At least I have a couple guys chasing me—more than I can say for her.

October 31

I spent some quality time with Laurita and her kitten today. She is such a bright child. Her English is coming along very well. Laurita is teaching her father everything I teach her. Juanita speaks English but rarely speaks to anyone. I wish she would go to an anger-management class.

Marla and I passed out a million pieces of candy to trick-or-treaters tonight. Where do they all come from? We dressed Laurita up in a princess costume.

November 1

My car wouldn't start this morning—made me late for Rose Club. Ricky said a wire came loose. Good as new. Kirby drools every time he sees my Porsche. I told him he could have it when I die. He laughed.

November 2

Woke up coughing, runny nose. I stayed home all day, finished reading *Nothing to Envy*. Wow, what a read! I'm exhausted. Pedro presented me with a beautiful handmade cutting board. He is very good with wood.

November 3

This year is really flying by. Worked in the garden until a cold wind came up. Started a murder mystery by Barbara Jean Coast. Feeling better today. Karen left a message for my dental appointment. Buzz called.

November 4

I woke up last night—thought I heard scraping sounds outside my window. Couldn't go back to sleep so I got up and read. Juanita didn't get home from work till three in the morning.

November 5

Went to church this morning. Marla stayed home from work with a headache. Kirby was here when I got back. The three of us had lunch and played cards for a couple hours. Need to make a hair appointment.

November 6

As soon as Marla went to work, Pedro came to the back door to ask for more medicine. He pleaded until I thought I would cry. I gave him enough for this week. He obviously didn't cut back yet, but he will have to. I'm so thankful I don't have to take pain pills any more.

November 7

Buzz drove me down to Monterey for the Seabird Festival. We had a great time until it started raining. We had lunch at the wharf and came home early. I heard hammering noises in the garage?

November 8

I was late to my doctor appointment because the car wouldn't start—again! Ricky said a wire was loose again. I told him to tighten it. Doc saw me late—didn't look happy. He was very reluctant to renew my prescription.

November 9

Mel's room is finally finished. He will move in as soon as he has time. I think it will be nice having him here, living on the old homestead. Mom and Dad would have approved.

November 10

Laurita fell on the patio and skinned her knee this morning. No one answered the door—pretty sure her mom was still asleep. The night shift is a killer. I cleaned and bandaged the knee. Such a sweet girl.

November 11

Kirby came over for dinner. Apparently Marla invited him. Nobody told me. I helped with the cooking but I let Marla clean up afterwards. Kirby went to the kitchen and helped her. I don't remember him ever doing that for me. Grrrr.

November 12

There was frost all over the lawn this morning. Laurita's kitty was out all night. Poor little thing was half froze when I picked her up. Mel moved a few of his things into the garage this evening.

November 13

I planted the rose bush Buzz gave me for my birthday. It was root-bound in the pot. Now I will think of Buzz every time I see the rose bush; not sure if that's a good thing.

November 14

Ricky tried to sell me some firewood. I told him we don't use the fireplace very often. Caught him drooling over my car this afternoon. I wonder if he's still going to school. I think he's basically a good kid; too bad his home-life is so bad.

November 15

Claudia called to ask when the next painting class was happening. I told her it is tomorrow. I'm looking forward to it. Something I like to do. But I love to knit too. So much fun—so little time.

November 16

Kati drove us to Pacific Grove to paint. It was a beautiful day with huge white clouds. I really enjoyed painting them, and the smooth green water. It was pretty warm for November. Everyone thought so. Marla's painting was outstanding.

November 17

Marla is so touchy—can't talk to her. Buzz called last night. He wants me to see what he painted Saturday, as if I didn't see it or hear about it all day. He's not a bad painter, actually. He just talks too much.

November 18

Five weeks until the Aromas Art Festival. I'm already excited. Buzz said he wants to be in it this year. What he really wants is to share my space. And what he really, really wants is to take over my space. It took years to get it and I'm keeping it.

November 19

Laurita knocked on my back door this morning. She hadn't had any breakfast. You would think Pedro could help her, feed her once in awhile. He can get around with the wheelchair I bought him. I'm beginning to think he just doesn't care. I wonder if he's depressed.

November 20

Went to my dental appointment today. Sometimes I think it would be easier and cheaper to just yank the teeth out. But I'll keep them as long as I can. Marla sure seems happy about something?

November 21

Shopped in Santa Cruz today with Laurita. Pedro asked me to babysit her so I took her with me. We had so much fun. Later we stopped off in Capitola to watch the waves. On the news they said they were 18 feet—I believe it! Juanita was angry that we were so late.

November 22

My car wouldn't start again. I'm so upset. Ricky fixed it, but why is this happening over and over? Looking forward to a great paint day tomorrow. The weather report says it will be blustery with high waves.

My eyes stung. Mary had said she was looking forward to the paint day. Too bad she didn't get sick and stay home that day.

I pushed the journal into my purse, climbed out of the truck and padded over to the hospital. I asked about Marla at the nurse's station. A friendly little nurse pointed down the hall to Room 150. I found Marla snuggled under a thin blanket, plugged into an IV, sound asleep. I gave her shoulder a tug.

"What, oh, Josephine, what are you doing here?"

"Just wanted to give you this." I put the book on the side table. "How do you feel?"

"I was dreaming about salad…actually, I don't remember anything after I left your house. How did you know I was here?"

"I went looking for you."

Marla wrinkled her eyes. "Huh?"

"I helped the officer get you out of your car. Just lucky we found you."

"Thank you, Josephine, I think?" She rolled over and closed her eyes.

That night I dreamt I was Steve McQueen driving a little blue Porsche through acres of slippery lettuce plants, swerving and fish-tailing all over the place until I finally found a steep hill. The car stopped, I climbed out and realized I was standing on railroad tracks. A loud horn warned me that a train was very close.

Chapter 12

Last week Alicia and I had made plans to go to Sonia's yoga class Wednesday. It was already Wednesday morning and I was so sleepy I could hardly pull myself out of bed. Besides, my new mattress was so, so comfortable. But I didn't want to let Alicia down so I scrambled into exercise clothes, grabbed a power bar and a cup of coffee and roared down San Juan Road. The morning sun shone on Marla's skid marks and a long swath of missing lettuce. I wondered how she was doing. Would she like a visit?

I drove to the lake district of Watsonville, parked in front of Alicia's house and read a note posted on the front door.

"Jo, I tried to call you but remembered that you don't answer your cell phone when you drive. I'm sorry I can't make it to yoga today, Ernie and Trigger are on Christmas break and they wanted to go to the snow. Did you know that it snowed in Tahoe yesterday and it's snowing today? We're coming home Friday because Trigger has a birthday party to go to. I packed my paints and paper. See you soon. Allie."

I smiled at the thought of Trigger flapping his arms up and down in the snow making snow angels. I decided to skip yoga and visit Marla instead. As I cruised through the hospital parking lot, I saw several of my friends heading for the side entrance leading to the room where yoga lessons were held twice a week.

But I parked near the main entrance, between a beautiful blue Porsche and a manly white Mustang.

Marla's admirers were swarming.

The show started even before I had time to climb out of my truck. A red-headed gal with an old guy on each arm walked cautiously toward the parking area. The guys were in a heated discussion. I couldn't make out the words, only the attitude. At one point Marla saw me and stopped walking. She said something to the men and they obediently walked her over to my truck.

"Marla," I said as I slammed the truck door behind me. "How are you feeling…?"

"Josephine, would you mind driving me home?" Her lower lip trembled.

"Sure, no problem."

Kirby helped her up into the passenger seat and handed over a white plastic bag big enough to hold her purse, the journal and several pages of doctor's instructions. I buckled myself in and turned the key. "Light on the luggage today?"

For a moment she looked at me like I was a bit touched, and then said, "Oh, you're right, no suitcase for me." She smiled. "They say I'm lucky to be alive."

"Yeah, that was some Evil Knievel stunt you performed last night. Any word on how your car is doing?"

"No, but I'll have to deal with it when I get home."

I didn't think she looked strong enough to deal with anything right away, especially Moe and Larry, better known as Buzz and Kirby.

"I hope you're planning to stay home from work for a while."

"Yes, I might do that. I haven't really thought it through, you see." She pressed her right hand over the left to keep it from shaking, kind of a subconscious thing she often did. We drove south toward Capitola in silence. Marla dropped her head back against the headrest and closed her eyes. I hated to disturb her once we were parked in front of her house.

"Oh my," she exclaimed, "I must have dosed off. Thank you for driving me home, Josephine." She popped her seatbelt open and started to climb down from her seat. I was already there at the curb to catch her if she teetered. She wobbled up to the front porch. I carried the shopping bag with one hand and steadied her elbow with the other. She fished around in her purse for the house key, found it and opened the door.

"Do you need me for anything?" I asked.

"No, you've been wonderful. Thank you, Josephine." She disappeared into the house.

Walking back to my truck, I heard the front door open. I turned.

"Josephine…." Marla's eyes were big, her mouth open, but no more words came out.

I walked swiftly back to the porch.

"What's going on? You look like you saw…."

"Josephine, someone's been in my house," she whispered.

"Maybe it was Mel."

"No, Mel would never track mud into the house." We crept from room to room, all the way to the kitchen. "Look at this mess! Someone obviously ate my leftover steak from the California Grill, and look, there's a dirty plate and a glass with some milk in it. Mel would never do this."

"Does anyone have a key?"

"Just Mel…and there's a key under the potted geranium on the porch."

"Who knows about it?"

"I don't know. I don't go around telling everyone about it." She peeked into the guest bath and shivered. I never leave this open." Marla pointed to the mirror door of a medicine cabinet above the sink. "Mary kept her medicines in here…I could have sworn there were more bottles than this, but I never actually counted them. In fact, I was planning to throw those old prescriptions away. It's just so scary to think someone went all through my house. I wonder what else they did."

"Let's call 911," I suggested.

"I'm so tired. But you're right, we must call."

I found her phone in the kitchen and punched in the three magic numbers. I handed the phone to Marla, who gave the 911 operator a genuinely emotional description and reaction to the break-in. While waiting for the police to arrive, we inspected the house all over again. This time Marla noticed a couple open drawers in Mary's bedroom—not open much, just a half inch or so. But she said everything had been in perfect order when she left home. I already knew she was not the type to leave home with a drawer open.

I searched the cupboards for food and heated up a couple bowls of Campbell's chicken noodle soup for lunch because, as a child, I had learned that the soup would fix everything. At least I believed it would. And sure enough, an idea came to me as we sipped our soup.

"Marla, I think you should invite Mel to sleep in Mary's room a few nights to help you feel safe."

"I'm afraid our relationship is a bit strained. Mel thinks Mary and I favored the Herreras over him. But it wasn't as simple as that. Mary saw the family struggling and wanted to help and I went along with it. It had nothing to do with Mel."

"Maybe this will change his mind—bring him closer to you."

"Would you do the asking, Josephine?"

"Sure, but I think we should go together on it. He needs to know it's coming from you. When he sees how…ah…distressed you are…."

"I look that bad?" She bit her lower lip.

"You look pretty good considering all you've been through," I said, diplomatically.

The door bell rang.

Marla opened the door. A policewoman showed her badge and walked into the house. Marla took her on a tour of the three rooms where her things had been disturbed. The officer was a little worried about the missing pills but in the end she recommended getting an alarm system. When she drove away, I found myself in a dilemma. Should I go home and paint, or stay with Marla?

"Marla, I have an idea to take your mind off this break-in."

"What's on your mind?"

"I think we should paint together, you know, each do a watercolor painting. Wouldn't that be fun?"

"Well, it might take my mind off…."

"Yeah, it'll be good therapy for you. Where do you keep the paint? Mary's room?"

She nodded and I headed for the bedroom. Minutes later, I came back to the kitchen with a box of paints, brushes and a large tablet of watercolor paper. We settled in at the dining room table, stared at our blank pieces of paper and waited for an idea to pop.

Marla stood up and walked to the kitchen. She returned holding a wall calendar. We looked at chicken pictures from January to December and decided to paint the magnificent Silver-Gray Dorking rooster posing on the roof of a wire brooding box full of chicks.

"I'm x-ing the box of chicks," I said. "Too difficult for my level of watercolor expertise."

"I see what you mean. Maybe I'll just paint a few of those chicks and forget the rooster," Marla chuckled like it was a joke.

"By the way, Marla, why did Mary need pain pills?"

Marla opened her mouth, nothing came out. She put her brush in water and sucked in some air. "Kind of warm in here, don't you think?" She opened a window and came back to her painting. "Mary had knee replacement surgery about three years ago. Like many people, she became addicted to her pain pills. She was determined to get off them, but couldn't do it. The night she crashed into the Herrera car, she had taken pills and drank some wine."

"Oh, that explains her feelings of guilt…."

"Yes it does, but it shook her up so badly she never took another pill."

"But I found a bottle of her pills that dropped out of Mel's pocket when he fell off my roof."

"Actually, I knew her prescription was being refilled, but I didn't know the pills were going to my brother." Her chin dropped, eyes focused on the table top.

"Do you think Mel would be more likely to tell me about it, or tell you?"

"I don't think he would tell me, knowing how much I was against Mary taking pills."

"Okay, I'll go talk to him before I go home. Your chicks are coming along nicely."

"Thank you, Josephine. Mary was nuts over chickens. Know anyone who would like a few chicken nick-knacks?"

"Maybe you should take them to the festival and give them to the person who buys your chick painting." We laughed.

I enjoyed painting with Marla. She told me about her social worker stuff and I talked about some of the more unusual murals I had painted. She said she would turn sixty-five in January, and dreaded having to retire. I tried to convince her that painting might become a second career, sighting Whistler's mother as an example.

"Good try, Josephine, but James Whistler wasn't as old as I when he painted a picture of his mother," she laughed. "But I understand your point."

It was six o'clock when I finally finished my painting. Marla finished hers much earlier. She suggested we get some dinner at Gayle's Bakery in the Capitola Village. I was starving and agreed we should go.

"But before we go, I want to talk to Mel," I said to Marla, and stepped out the back door, crossed the patio and knocked on the door that no one ever answered. I opened it and walked down the corridor to Mel's door. He opened his door before my fist hit the wood.

"Josephine, what's going on?"

"Did you know that your sister was in a terrible wreck last night?"

"You're kidding…right?" His face balled up into a mass of worry lines.

"Not kidding. Marla was mad at me when she left my house. Did you know that she drives too fast?"

"She's done that her whole life. How is she? Was she hurt?"

"She stayed the night at the Watsonville Hospital, but they let me drive her home this morning and I've been here all day. I think she would feel better if you stayed in the house with her for a night or two."

"I thought you said she was okay…."

"Yes and no. Her nerves are pretty shot. We walked through the house this morning and she said she saw mud on the floor, food missing, open drawers, that type of thing and figured someone had broken in. The police came, but there was nothing of value stolen so the officer advised her to get an alarm system."

"Jees, that's awful. I guess I'll sleep in Mary's old bed, if it's okay with Marla."

"I'm sure it's okay. Mel, do you take pain pills for anything?"

"That's a weird question."

"Do you?"

"Yeah, sometimes."

"You got them from Mary?"

"Yeah, she used to be addicted to them. She got clean about a year ago but she kept buying the pills for anyone who needed them. At least that's what she told me. I pulled a ligament in my leg. She let me have a bottle…nothing wrong with that."

"Thanks, Mel, didn't mean to go all personal on ya. I'm still looking for clues to your sister's murder. If you know anything…."

"I'm glad you're looking into it, Josephine. The cops were here once. Haven't heard a thing since. I think they gave up."

"If it's any comfort, I never give up. Hey, why don't you join Marla and me; we're going to get some dinner at Gayle's Bakery."

"Let me put on a clean shirt and I'll meet you in five minutes."

Mel drove us to Gayle's in his over-sized four-door truck. I was squished into the little back seat, but the delicious dinner was worth it. After dinner, Mel looked content, Marla looked tired and I felt sleepy.

As I drove my truck home I thought about the Quintanas spending time in Tahoe. As soon as Solow was fed, I called Alicia.

"Hi, Jo…."

"Hi, Allie, is it snowing up there?"

"Sure is. It was beautiful today."

"I wanted to tell you about Marla."

"What about Marla?"

"She was in the hospital…but she's all right now, I think. It's a long story…I sort of borrowed Mary's journal hoping it would help me solve her murder. Marla came to my house last night, saw the journal and went ballistic. I was real worried about her because she drove down my driveway so fast so I followed her. Sure enough, she crashed her car in a lettuce field. She doesn't remember any of it…."

"Jo, you're using your hobby as an excuse to do unethical things."

"I feel awful about it, but I wanted proof that Marla, Buzz and Vick were innocent. Then I read about Kirby…."

"How is Marla?" Alicia sounded impatient.

"She's fine. They let her leave the hospital this morning and I had dinner with her and Mel this evening. I found the diary and gave it back to her so I think we're on good terms at this point.

"Jo, try to behave while I'm gone," Alicia said in her "mother" voice.

"Sure, but tell Trigger to make a snow angel for me."

Chapter 13

Nine more days left until the festival. It was already Thursday, time to get serious about painting. Next week I planned to buy frames from Buzz and frame the pictures. If I finished a picture today, I would have five—one for David and four to sell. *Not too bad*, I thought. At last count, Alicia had thirteen, but who was counting?

After breakfast, I taped a paper to my board and started painting my view from the dining room windows. I saw a patch of bright green weeds, the front end of my sweet little red truck, a prissy white cat sitting on the hood and black clouds blowing in from the north. First, I used friskit in the space on the hood where the cat would be sitting. Then came the clouds, the truck and grass. Once everything was painted in, I erased the friskit and added a few shadows to her prissy whiteness. I named it, "Cat on a Hot Truck."

Five minutes after I finished the painting, I piled Solow into my "hot truck" and we took off for Marla's house in Capitola. I planned to stop in at Jake's apartment and get home in time to spend a quiet evening with David.

I remembered that Marla wasn't fond of dogs so I parked in the alley behind her house and left Solow on leash, tied to a fence post in the back yard. I found Marla and Laurita sitting in the sun. Marla was reading a storybook in English to the little girl who was all eyes, ears and joyful squeals.

Marla finished reading the last page and looked up. "Josephine, Nice to see you…."

"Hi, Marla and Laurita. That used to be my favorite story, *The Little Engine that Could.*

"Laurita, go wake up your mother, it's two o'clock."

The little girl ran into the garage and slammed the door.

"Now, what's happening with you, Josephine?"

"Mainly, I wanted to see how you're doing. You're looking back to normal today."

"Normal, but still worried about break-ins."

"Maybe you should get an alarm system," I suggested.

"That's what Mel's doing right now—shopping for one. He was a great comfort last night, just knowing he was in the house."

"Still no ideas about who broke in and why?"

"No, not really." Marla carried the storybook into the house. I followed. She told me about her car not starting three different times and Ricky fixing it each time. She put on a pot of coffee and brought out a plate of Girl Scout cookies.

"Didn't Mary have the same problem with her car?"

"I had forgotten about that. You're right, she did." Marla's eyes grew big. "Someone is doing things to our cars…who would do that?"

"Marla, if it happens again, ask Mel to look at your car. Maybe he'll see something the young man didn't see."

"Right now I don't have a car." Her right hand automatically kept a lid on the left hand's jitters. "I have to wait for the adjuster to tell me if it was totaled or not. They said I would get a loaner…should be delivered sometime today."

"Marla, I read some of—actually all—of your sister's diary, a whole year's worth, trying to figure out a motive for murder. One thing that stood out was the fact that Buzz and Kirby were in competition for Mary, and later on for you?"

"I really haven't read the journal yet, but, yes, there was a bit of male competition for my sister, but certainly not for me. The boys and I just played cards and such." Her cheeks looked pink. "You see, when Claudia and Buzz broke up, Buzz started buzzing around here looking for sympathy and later for company. At first, Mary felt flattered, but eventually she tired of his attention."

I finally decided I'd had enough of *Peyton Place*, excused myself from the table and stepped out the backdoor just as Laurita finished untying Solow. He bounded across the lawn and up the back steps.

Marla appeared at the door and gasped as Solow pushed his way into the kitchen looking for cookie crumbs. I stepped on the dragging leash. He looked up at me wondering why I'd put a stop to his fun. I said goodbye to Marla and Laurita, walked Solow out the back door and across the back lawn to the truck and hefted him into his seat.

I drove the zig-zag course of jewel-named streets, made a right on Bay, cruised down the hill, crossed over a bridge leading into the village-half of Capitola and turned left into a neighborhood of small apartment houses. After a bit of circling, I finally slipped into a parking spot. The afternoon was warming up so I took Solow with me on leash to Jake's apartment. A note on the door referred us to the beach just two blocks away. We walked the dirt path along the river bank, crossed the main street of town and finished our walk on the congested esplanade where all the restaurants compete with each other for tourist business.

Solow and I sat on the beach for half an hour squinting into the sun, watching a very tall surfer teaching a group of two young girls and three boys how to surf. Even with his hair wet and slicked back, I knew it was Jake. When the class finally ended, Jake carried his board and towel across the sand to the cement bench where I sat and Solow slept.

"Nice dog ya got there. Got my message, did ya?"

"Actually, no...." I stood up and we started walking back to his apartment.

"It's not good news, I'm afraid. Had a break-in last night. Only thing missin' is the phone."

"You mean the phone?"

"Yep, that little bugger. I was out for a mug of amber fluid at the pub down the street. Maybe I forgot to lock up...not sure. Only reason I know someone was in my place is because my bird was goin' bonkers. Had his top feathers up and he's pacin' the top of the cage and there's feathers all over the floor. I looked round, nothing missing except the phone. I'm really sorry, Josephine..." he said as he opened the door to his apartment and ushered us in.

Solow growled softly as the hair down the middle of his back raised up. He must have sensed my anguish, or maybe he was distressed over the bird that was fluffed and pacing nervously. I felt prickles all over my body. I was flooded with questions about Mary's killer. Had he been right there in the room with the bird?. How did the killer know where to find the phone in the first place? Was I being followed? My legs felt weak. I sat down in Jake's desk chair without invitation.

"Doin' okay, Josephine? Ya look a bit pale, there."

Solow sensed my misery and whined.

"It's all right, big guy," I said to Solow, still holding his leash. I stood up. "We have to go now, Jake." I didn't say, "You idiot, why didn't you lock your stupid door?" But I sure wanted to. Jake was a nice young man and I could see that he felt bad enough already. But all the way home I bad-mouthed Jake until my anger finally subsided.

Solow slept. No grudges for him. I parked in front of my house. Like an over-tired child, Solow twitched, snored and slept on. I finally woke him and tried to talk him down from his seat. He just looked at me with sleepy, blood-shot eyes. I lifted his very solid body, and set him down gently on the driveway. Mr. Sleepy-head followed me into the house.

The sun had disappeared over the horizon, leaving the house dark and cold. I flipped on several lights, turned up the thermostat and poured kibble for Solow. I noticed a new message on my very retro answering machine and pushed the play button. The voice was easy to identify by the accent.

"G'day, Josephine, got the good and the bad news. The good bein' that I recovered three numbers…local, I believe. I'll pass them along to ya later…couldn't get to the pictures. The phone was stolen is the bad news."

I immediately called Jake and asked for the three phone numbers.

"Sorry, Josephine, I was about to tell you but you took a walkabout. Upset, you were." I wrote the numbers down as he read them to me.

"I'm okay now, and thanks for the numbers. How much do I owe you?"

"Not a Quid. I'm given ya the mate's discount for bodgy work. My fault the phone is gone."

"Thank you, Jake. Sorry I was short with you."

"No worries." He hung up.

I immediately called the first number. A canned recording asked for a message. The second number was a busy signal and the third number picked up quickly.

"We don't want any, and stop calling!" Dial tone.

I punched in the number a second time. Before the woman had time to open her mouth, in one big breath I quickly told her my name, phone number, asked her to call me when she had time and hung up before she could hang up on me.

Curiosity set in and she called. "Hello?"

"Hi, like I said, my name is Josephine and a couple people gave me phone numbers and my desk is kinda' messy…then I saw your number but there wasn't a name with it so I decided to just call on the chance you are the person I wanted to…."

"Okay, I get the picture. My name is Rona."

"Thank you, Rona. Do you happen to know Mary Milford?"

"Well, not any more. She's dead, you know."

"How did you know her?"

Big sigh. "She was my neighbor…is this call for a purpose? Did you know Mary? What's this about anyway?"

"I was Mary's friend and I'm trying to figure out how I got your number. You live on Jade Street?"

"Yeah, I gotta' go; someone's knockin' on the door…."

My next call was to Marla. She said the only Rona she knew was Ricky's mom who lived next door. I shuddered. So whoever owned the phone had made calls to Mary's neighbor. My next question to Marla was, "What did Mary's phone look like?" Her answer surprised me.

"It was a regular-looking phone, but Mary bought a red case for it to match her red purse because she was a Republican and my phone has a blue case because I'm a Democrat." Marla laughed. "I know it's silly, but sometimes we did silly things, you know, to make light of our different philosophies…making it easier to get along with each other. As different as we were, we managed rather well. I certainly do miss Mary."

"One more question—was Mary's phone in her purse the day she, ah, fell off the cliff?"

"She always kept it in her purse, but a couple days after she fell, I checked her purse and the phone wasn't there and I haven't found it anywhere. Maybe she was holding it, taking pictures when she fell."

"Will you be home tomorrow?" I asked Marla.

"I'll be home all day. Did I tell you I took the rest of the week off? My supervisor told me I should take two weeks, but I think I just need a few days to work out my aches and pains."

"I didn't know you were in pain…."

"It's okay, Josephine, not that bad for being in a car wreck, and Mary's pills work very well."

"I thought they were stolen…."

"All but the bottle I had in the top drawer of my bed stand," she chuckled.

"If you don't mind, I'd like to come over tomorrow morning so we can look at some new information…."

"That would be fine. I can't wait to see what you have."

We decided I would be there at noon. I hung up, poured a can of chili beans into a pot and heated it up, hoping a hot meal would soothe my nerves. Even the after-dinner ice cream didn't calm my over-active mind. My brain jumped from one phone number to the next and back to Rona. I picked up the phone and tried the first number Jake had given me. It rang three times.

"Hello?" The voice sounded like a young male.

"Hi, my name is Josephine. Sorry, I forgot your name…."

"Like, do you want to talk to my mom?"

"That depends, what's her name?"

"Rona. Who are you anyway?"

I hung up on Ricky and punched in the second phone number, the one that had a busy signal the last time I tried it.

"Sunny Senior Home," an overly cheerful female chirped.

"Sorry, I have the wrong number." I hung up, pulled out my phone book for Santa Cruz County and looked up Sunny Senior Home. The address was 288 Bain, Capitola. My heart skipped a couple beats. Another Capitola phone number! I spread a Santa Cruz County map on the kitchen table and quickly located Bain, just five blocks from Marla's house. I was dying to ask Marla if she knew anything about the senior home, but decided to wait until the next day when we would get together, besides, someone was at the back door.

David walked into my kitchen.

"The front door was locked," he said, cocking his head to one side. "You're always taking off, leaving it unlocked. Now, when you're home you lock it?"

"I know this neighborhood is safe," I sputtered, "but I just felt a little creepy when the sun went down…never mind."

"If it's any comfort, I just rescued Myrtle. I put water in the bucket. She lost a lot of needles but I think she'll make it till Christmas. I found this in your shed."

"Oh, good, you found the tree stand. Does it come with a service agreement and a guarantee?" I pressed.

"Very funny. I was planning to set up the tree for you. Anything else I can do?"

"Stick around; I'll make the popcorn." I winked.

Chapter 14

My Fridays typically involved dinner at the Quintanas, but I hadn't heard a word from Alicia. It was eleven o'clock, Friday morning. I figured they were probably at least half-way home from Tahoe, why hadn't she called? A second later, the phone rang.

"Hi, Jo; we're having a late breakfast at the lodge, and Trigger and Ernie plan to snowboard for a couple hours. We'll grab some dinner on the way home."

"Sounds like you're having a great time."

"Actually, I stay inside mostly and paint. I finished two paintings and I'm going to start another one while the boys are out having fun. I sit here at a desk by the window and paint the slopes, the skiers and the trees covered in snow. I'm having a great time."

"So you have about thirty paintings now?"

She laughed. "I think I have fifteen, but I'll only frame the best ones."

"I started a new painting early this morning and I'm almost finished," I said. "All I have to do is add shadows to the foxes."

"The what? It sounded like you said foxes…." Her cell phone crackled.

"I did. I copied a family of foxes from David's calendar. It has beautiful nature scenes. Allie, we only have one week left to get our art show together. Do you think we should go to yoga Monday?"

"Let's talk about it Sunday."

"Okay, bye."

I looked up at the clock on the wall and knew I would be late for my meeting with Marla. I tried calling her but Mel answered the house phone. He said she was running an errand and would be back by twelve. I told him to tell his sister I might not make it by twelve but I would try. Since the weather was unpredictable, I left Solow in the house. He whimpered when I left. If only Marla liked dogs. As I drove to Capitola, black clouds pushed south across a leaden sky. With so many trips to the little beach town, my already diminished rainy-day-fund was being burned up in the gas tank.

I cruised through the jewel neighborhood and curbed the truck behind Marla's black SUV loaner. Mel's truck wasn't around and neither was Mel. Marla answered the door with a flourish, as if she expected something grand. My three phone numbers didn't impress her.

"Marla, the interesting thing about these numbers is that they all come from this neighborhood. Do you know anything about the Sunny Senior Home?"

"Not really, except for the fact that Juanita works there. I don't know what she does; I just know she rides her bike over there every day at two-thirty in the afternoon and comes home around midnight, sometimes later."

"How long has she worked there?"

"Over a year. She has worked long enough to have seniority, so starting in January she gets Fridays and Saturdays off." Marla looked at the ceiling to see if she had forgotten anything. "And, of course, they like Juanita because she speaks Spanish. Her English is good, except for the accent of course. Pedro is trying hard to learn English, but it's not been easy for him."

"And then there's Ricky and his mom. What are they like?"

She thought for a moment. "I don't know Rona very well, but I know she works as a ranger at Seacliff

Beach. And Ricky graduated from high school last June, but I think he just hangs around the house…not sure what he does all day. The father's been gone since Ricky was two years old, poor kid. He's always helping me with things, as long as I pay him."

We sat at the kitchen table surrounded by yellow walls and chickens and roosters of every stripe. Even the toaster had a rooster decal pasted on its side. I tried to concentrate on the three phone numbers coming from a beat-up silver phone with no cover.

"Josephine…Josephine, would you like a cup of tea?" Marla asked.

"Oh, sure, that would be nice." Baffled, I ran each number through my mind over and over. Ricky and Rona landed at the top of my suspect list, but I could come up with no obvious reason for the boy or his mother to push Mary off the cliff. Rona had sounded edgy on the phone—sort of irritated with me, and Marla said Ricky had a bit of an attitude. But he was young.

Marla poured the tea and set a plate of brownies on the table. I wasn't shy about eating my share since it was lunchtime and my breakfast had happened very early that morning.

"Josephine, don't you think it's odd that Mary's car frequently broke down and my car was doing the same thing before it crashed? We both depended on Ricky, I guess, because he was always home and looking for odd jobs. He seemed to know what he was doing…."

"Marla, what if Ricky was sabotaging the cars and then getting paid to fix them?"

Marla's jaw dropped. "You might be on to something, Josephine. When I get my car back I'll ask Mel to fix anything that goes wrong."

"I have an idea; when Mel installs the alarm system have him install a camera on the front porch. Then we'll see if someone is tampering with the cars."

Feeling pleased with my idea, I glanced out the window. Mel was parking his truck across the street for lack of a better place. "Speak of the devil…."

"Josephine, I'm so glad you suggested that my little brother stay with me. I hope Mel will accept my invitation to live in the house with me until he gets back on his feet. It's so nice having him here."

"Nice having me?" Mel poked his head around the corner and laughed. "Hello, Josephine. Any news from your insurance company?"

"Just this check that came in the mail yesterday." I pulled an envelope out of my purse and waved it at him. He tried to grab it with his braced hand. I pulled it out of reach, all the while laughing and wishing I had a brother like Mel.

"Should I tell Mel what we know so far?" Marla asked.

I nodded. After all, Mel wasn't on my "most wanted" list. At least not yet.

He ripped the envelope and pulled out his check. He told us it was enough money to keep him going for another month and pay all the hospital bills. He turned to go.

"Going to the bank?" Marla asked.

"Yeah, anything you need while I'm out?"

"Pick up a security camera, would you please? I'll give you some money…." She stood up to go get her purse.

"No, you won't. This is on me, Sis. I was planning to get a camera even before you mentioned it. There's something going on in this neighborhood."

We watched Mel, still wearing his big black boot, cross the street and climb awkwardly into his truck. Marla smiled, looking proud of her younger brother. She said she would talk to him later about the neighbors and our theory concerning cars that break down during the night.

I thought to myself, *What if Mary had figured out what Ricky was doing and threatened to tell his mother or the police?* Perhaps there was a motive for murder in that scenario. I cautioned Marla not to mention our theory to Ricky or Rona. We would play dumb until we had absolute proof.

"Marla, it's none of my business, but what did Mary do for a living?"

She laughed, "Mary was the oldest child so naturally she inherited the house and a nice lump sum of money. She sold her ice cream shop on Ocean Street three years ago and retired."

Marla finally noticed the brownies were gone and brought out a plate of cheese and crackers. She refilled our mugs with hot tea and sat down. "You don't know how good it feels to not be going to work. I used to love the work, now it's just *work*!"

"How long until you can retire?"

"Two years ago. I have plenty of time in, but just can't make up my mind. What would I do all day?"

"Everyday would be like today," I said. You just do things you want to do, visit, travel, relax, walk to the beach, play with Laurita, paint…."

"You make it all sound so good. I'll think about it some more." She munched a cracker, staring straight ahead, focused on her future.

Suddenly a little girl's scream broke the silence.

Marla moved across the room like a twenty-year-old instead of a sixty-year-old.

I followed her out the back door to the patio where Laurita stood holding her kitten against her chest, drenching the little guy in tears. Marla sat down on the last concrete step and put her arms out. Laurita fell into her embrace, kitty half squashed in the middle.

"Laurita, dear, what's wrong?"

She gulped some air and whispered, "Kitty got no cola."

"Cola?" Marla pushed the girl back and took a look at the cat. "What happened to Kitty's tail?" she gasped. "Who did this?"

I stepped closer to see. "Oh my…what happened to the poor thing?"

Laurita carried the kitten across the patio and a stretch of lawn, to a wooden fence separating the Milford property from Rona's back yard. She held kitty as high as a five-year-old could reach against the fence, then clenched the cat with both hands and swooped it down to the lawn. Kitty screamed. Laurita began crying again.

Marla and I looked at each other—we got the message. Marla looked ready to kill. I felt like helping her.

Marla stretched her arms out and Laurita ran to her, burying kitty in the folds of Marla's sweater. "Dear, tell us who did this…."

Tears welled up in Laurita's dark eyes. It was clear to everyone that we needed to go next door and have a talk with Ricky, and his mother if she was home. Marla informed me that the ranger business kept her away from home for long hours. We trudged through Marla's house, out the front door and over to Rona's front porch.

Ricky answered the door.

Marla stepped closer to the boy. He looked down at her while Laurita hid behind Marla's legs, still holding Kitty. "Ricky, do you know anything about this?" Marla turned to give him a view of the kitten. "Half the cat's tail is missing!"

"Yeah, I know…it was kinda' my fault."

"How could you do such a thing?" Marla choked on her words.

"I was mowing the lawn and this kitten kept playing with the mower. It was attacking the machine with its front paws, and then it would run away, come back and attack and run away. I should have just shut the mower down and finished the lawn when the cat wasn't around. I just didn't think anything bad would happen…until it did." He hung his head. "I don't suppose it could be reattached?"

"I don't believe so," Marla said in a softer tone. "You need to apologize to Laurita for harming her kitten."

Ricky squatted down on his haunches. "I'm very sorry, Laurita. It was an accident."

The little girl wiped her eyes and peeked around Marla's mature frame. She gave Ricky a weak smile. "Que ac..cee..dent?"

"Something happened because I wasn't being careful," he said.

Laurita ducked back behind Marla.

I wondered where Laurita's mom was. With all the shrieking and hysterical crying, at least one parent should have made an appearance.

Ricky said he was sorry one more time and was rewarded with a tiny Laurita-smile.

I followed Marla and the little girl back to Marla's patio where we cleaned and wrapped Kitty's tail. Marla added a yellow ribbon tied in a bow and Laurita giggled.

I walked over to the garage side-door and opened it. Feeling angry, I knocked on the Herrera's door several times to no avail. An old bicycle leaned against the inner wall. I stepped around it, back onto the sunny patio and asked Marla who owned the bike.

"That old thing? Mary was going to take it to the Salvation Army, but Juanita said she wanted it. She rides it to work all the time, rain or shine. Today, she and Mr. Herrera are out walking, that is, she's pushing him in his wheelchair. They should be back soon." She glanced across the back lawn.

"You mean they went off and left Laurita here alone?" I snorted, arms folded across my chest.

"Not alone, she's with me." Marla smiled. "I don't mind at all. She's such a good little thing."

Out of the corner of my eye I saw something move. Two men walked up to the little wooden gate at the end of the lawn that faced the alley. They were a matched set, big, tall, each wearing the same dark uniform that turned out to be Mechanic's overalls. One man reached around and unlatched the gate.

"Ms. Milford?"

"Yes, that's me." Marla set Laurita onto her little feet, and stood up. "Can I help you?"

"Got some papers for you to sign. Car's out front."

"My car? Oh my, that was quick." She beamed.

"Did a little body work and paint and she's good to go," he said, as he handed her a pile of paperwork.

All I could think about was Hotrod Marla traveling who knows where at top speeds. I said a quick goodbye to Marla and Laurita. Even as I sped home, I knew I would be back. Camera or no camera, I wanted to see what would happen to Marla's SUV after dark.

It was only three in the afternoon when I entered my house. Myrtle greeted me with her piney fragrance. She looked so pretty next to the TV in the living room. I ignored my nostalgic feelings because I was starving and Solow needed lovin'. When the urgent stuff had been attended to, I pulled out my watercolor equipment and began a new painting—Laurita holding Kitty from memory.

From where I painted in the dinning room, I could easily see Myrtle, naked and alone. She longed to wear bling and lots of it. I made a mental note to check her water and bring down the old Christmas tree ornaments from the loft—later.

Chapter 15

I have always believed things happen for a reason. Was the Watercolor God testing me to see if I was a *real* artist, dedicated to my profession and true to the artistic principles revealed to me by my teachers and their teachers going all the way back to Michelangelo's time? If only I had confidence in my ability. Over the years I had achieved confidence when it came to creating murals of all types. Why did little bitty old watercolor paintings give my brain a rash? Why did the inscrutable medium cause me to panic and question my ability to paint?

It was Friday afternoon, soon to be Friday night, the sun was just about to plop into the Pacific and I had just finished another painting. But was it any good? I would find out at the Art Festival in just eight days. I had six pieces for the event and hoped to double that number by show-time.

I had successfully ignored David all afternoon by not answering phone calls and emails. I knew he would not approve of my plans for the evening, but Solow would be good company, always enjoying a new adventure. Not that this would be an adventure. I just wanted to see for myself if anything sneaky was going on in Marla's neighborhood.

I hefted Solow into the passenger seat of my truck and rounded the cab carrying my purse, a book, a jacket and a lap blanket. I climbed into the driver's seat. Solow howled, sensing a good ride as we headed north. Since most of the commuters coming home from work traveled south, we made pretty good time, arriving in Capitola and the Pacific Ocean a few minutes after sunset.

Solow's tail thumped the seat to the rhythm of the Beach Boys as I turned into the drive-through at Burger Queen. I bought enough burger food for at least three people and one hungry dog, plus two coffees. I parked the truck in a near-by Starbuck's parking lot and shared the food with Solow, leaving one burger wrapped for later. I sipped my coffee slowly, waiting for the stars to come out and maybe the moon. I hoped the moon would be just a sliver so that my truck would not be easily identified. Solow settled in for a nap and I read two chapters of *Death of a Dummy* by C. F. Carter. When I finally looked up from the book, it was dark—time to cruise over to the Jewel neighborhood.

I curbed the truck across the street and half a block east of Marla's house. The nearest streetlight was five car lengths from my stake-out position. It was almost eight o'clock and quiet as stardust. Marla's car and Mel's truck were parked in front of the house as usual. The Porsche was missing. A full blue-cheese moon climbed up from behind the house. Dim light shone from three of Marla's draped windows, as smoke curled into the evening chill from her fireplace. I wished I was inside eating popcorn, snuggled under a lap blanket with Solow at my feet.

Solow snorted, twitched his eyelids and dog-paddled his feet on the passenger seat. From where I sat, it looked like a fast and furious Fluffy chase. He was so cute, sleeping like a baby. If Marty hadn't been hit by an eighteen wheeler seventeen years ago, and if we had had a baby…a child to raise…would I still feel this way toward Solow?

I sipped cold coffee and draped the lap blanket over my Levis. With a pen-light I was barely able to see the print in the Carter mystery that had me in its clutches.

Mid-sentence, a door slammed.

Headlights smacked my windshield.

I ducked down.

Mel drove past me in his big black truck, heading toward town.

I yawned and checked my watch; it was eleven-thirty. Marla's Lexus looked clean and polished in the moonlight. Her house was dark except for the porch light. Ricky's house had a yellow glow coming from one small window. The rest of the houses were dark. I locked my doors when I saw someone wearing a long dark coat shuffling his slippers down the sidewalk while holding a leash attached to a large black dog. Minutes later, they passed my truck on their return trip.

Fully engaged in my mystery book for some time, I looked up when headlights glommed onto my windshield but quickly went dark. I watched Mel get out of his truck and stand in the road, hands on hips. He stood where Marla's car had been parked.

"Solow, stay. Sorry old boy." I said as I slammed the door and ran across the street.

"Josephine, what are you doing here?"

"I've been watching your sister's car, sort of, to see if anyone tampered with it…."

"Did you see who took the car?"

"I'm afraid not; I was reading this really good mystery…."

"Okay, I get the picture. I can't believe it got stolen. Get in my truck and we'll look around, see if we can spot it." Mel was already in his seat by the time I opened the passenger door. I finally got my seatbelt buckled as we turned onto Forty-First Avenue. The normally busy main street of Capitola looked pretty quiet at twelve-thirty in the morning.

Truck tires squealed around the corner and Mel shot through a yellow-going-red light. He drove awfully fast for a guy wearing a Velcro boot and a wrist brace. His jaw was set, his face an angry red. I wished I could go home. It was something about other people driving too fast. I needed to feel in control, but that wasn't going to happen, so I gripped the edge of the seat and let the big old Dodge suck gas like a jetliner all the way to the end of Forty-First Avenue—all the way to Soquel.

"Do you have a plan?" I asked, feeling a little green around my edges.

"Nope, do you?"

I shook my head in shame. I had had my head in a book and wasn't even aware of someone stealing the SUV. If the thief had hot-wired the car, I should have noticed, I should have heard something. If only I had looked up. I bit my lip out of frustration.

Mel hung a hard left U-turn and we headed back down Forty-First Avenue toward the ocean. When the ocean came into view, he parked at the cliffs and honked the horn with his forehead.

"Take it easy, Mel. We'll call the police when we get back."

"You can call right now—use your cell phone," he grumped. "This is all my fault, I should have installed the camera today."

"Maybe we should wait until morning to call the police so we won't have to wake up Marla," I yawned. "Boy is she gonna' be grumpy!"

"Would you like a hot cup of coffee and a burger or something? I could sure use a burger," he said, his good hand clenched into a fist.

"I'm not really hungry, but I would love a cup of coffee."

Mel fired up the engine and cruised back up Forty-First to the Burger Queen drive-thru. We ordered and ate in the warm cozy atmosphere of the truck. Mel gave me half his fries to go with my coffee. He polished off two double burgers in record time. Pent-up anger had given him quite an appetite.

"Hey, Mel, look at that car over there at the taco place." I pointed at a white SUV across six lanes of the main street. We watched the car cut across a parking area and six empty lanes, heading west on Forty-First Avenue.

Mel choked on a fry and spilled his mega icy drink on his lap. "Yoweee—x, x, x!"

"Hurry, he's getting away!" I shouted. "Looked like a guy wearing a hoody."

Mel handed me what was left of his burger and fries, and started up the engine. He jammed his sore foot to the floor board. My head whipped back, only to whip forward half a block away at a red stop-light. We had to stop for the next two red lights and barely made it through a couple yellows. By the time we got down to the Jewel district there were no other cars in sight. Mel sighed and cussed under his breath.

We roared all the way to the end of Forty-First Avenue and turned around at the cliffs where we'd parked earlier in the evening. Red-faced Mel morphed into quiet Mel as he drove his truck slowly back to the Jewel neighborhood and turned right at Jade Street. We cruised along, feeling defeated and hopeless. The whole neighborhood was dark except for Marla's porch light, a few street lights and a big silver moon overhead.

Mel slowed the truck and parked it at the curb behind a white SUV.

"What the heck?" he shouted at the moon as he climbed out of his seat.

"Did we just imagine it was stolen?" I jumped down from my seat, rounded the truck and looked at Mel. He looked at me. Even the moon was smiling. Solow woke up and howled from inside my truck parked across the street half a block away.

"Guess we're both crazy!" Mel laughed, as he picked me up and swung me in a circle. His face had softened in the moonlight, his eyes twinkled and his lips were on mine.

Chapter 16

When the sun came up Saturday morning I was still wondering if Mel and I had made the right decision. If my truck had been stolen I would want to know about it, but in the wee hours of the morning we decided we would spare Marla the shock. Besides, the car had been returned. Everything was all right, and Mel promised he would install the camera first thing in the morning.

Along with the stolen vehicle, I had a perfect memory of a Friday night kiss, but refused to re-run it in my mind. It was nothing, just a joyful moment, a mindless reaction to circumstances. I was sure Mel never gave it a second thought. Guys went around kissing people all the time. They learn it in junior high and never stop.

In an attempt to stop my brain from whirling out of control, I crawled out of bed and into the shower. But Ms. Brain continued twirling me into the land of hot flashes as I dried my hair. Solow brought me back to reality with a wet nose to my calf. I followed him to the back door and let him out just as David was coming in.

"Sorry, I thought you'd be up by now," he said with a grin, eyeing the fluffy white towel wrapped around my full figure.

"Yeah, well, it was a late night. Marla's car was stolen. Mel and I went looking for it and when we got back, there was her car. Craziest thing!"

"I came over to see if you wanted to go to breakfast with me, but maybe we should do lunch instead."

"That sounds wonderful. Come back in an hour." I closed the door behind him, hurried back to the bathroom and finished up my beauty routine. I zipped up my best black jeans and pulled on a soft white sweater. Before my hour was up, I put on the coffee maker, tossed sheets into the washing machine, dusted and vacuumed the living room and pulled a roast out of the freezer for dinner.

David showed up on schedule. He sat down at the kitchen table and began reading a newspaper he'd brought with him. I spontaneously pushed the paper away, sat on his lap and pressed my lips to his. Not that I wanted to compare kissers, but it did cross my mind. As I'd thought, there was no comparison. David was the Kissing King.

"What's this all about?" he laughed.

"Just feeling grateful for our friendship," I said, as my cheeks burned. I stood up and poured him a cup of coffee, feeling his eyes on me as I pulled clean dishes out of the dishwasher and put them away.

"I was thinking we might run down to Monterey and have lunch on the wharf," he said.

"That sounds wonderful. What's the occasion?"

"Exactly ten years since the day of the big storm. Remember, a tree fell and my Jeep was caught under the power lines…?"

"And I came along and called for help. I can't believe it's been ten years since…."

"My wife ran off with the preacher," he finished my thought. "Don't worry, I can say it without any ill effects," he laughed.

"Just one thing; it's Saturday and the traffic will be horrific. Maybe we should head north instead. Capitola has some great restaurants."

David looked through me like I was a window. He knew I had an ulterior motive to go to Capitola, but he went along with my wishes. Not sure of the weather, we loaded light jackets and heavy coats into the Jeep plus two pairs of flip-flops in case it warmed up and we wanted to walk on the beach. David shoveled Solow into the back seat on top of the coats. We buckled up and David drove his sweet old Jeep down the driveway. Just as we were about to enter Otis, he slammed on the brakes, sending Solow to the floor.

At the same time, a little blue car had turned off Otis and started up the driveway. The driver stomped on his brakes. The car fish-tailed, spitting gravel as it spun around and jolted to a stop just inches from our bumper. The Porsche engine sputtered and died.

David turned off the engine and walked over to the classic blue Porsche 911 and leaned down to Kirby's open window.

"Hey, old man, are you lost?"

"Hey, Davey, old buddy, thought I'd stop by and say hi."

"Just happens we're on our way to Capitola for lunch. Like to join us?"

"Already had my lunch, thanks anyway." Kirby started up the engine, revved it, reversed onto Otis, popped it into first gear and took off toward Aromas.

My shoulders relaxed as he drove away.

David hopped back into the Jeep and we enjoyed a lovely drive until he asked me what really happened the night before. Apparently, he hadn't believed my stolen car story and I hadn't even mentioned my intentions to do it all over again, night after night, until I figured out who was doing what with Marla's car. I couldn't help feel that the car problems had something to do with the murder, since Mary's car had also been affected. People don't just fall off cliffs for no reason, and cars don't just disappear.

"I'm sorry, Josie, don't mind me. You know how I worry about you. Just promise you'll be careful, okay?" he said as we roared north on Highway One.

"I'm sorry I worried you," I said. We were approaching my favorite view of the ocean. "I'll be careful, David…oh look at the water, it looks like a sheet of polished silver."

We passed the Aptos exits and took the Bay Street turn off. David's Jeep zipped into a parking space near the esplanade, an amazing victory for any Saturday afternoon. Gazing out the windshield, the beach looked clean, no signs of storm refuse, just sparkling sand, a calm sea and a grey bank of fog marking the horizon. People were everywhere. No matter what the weather, tourists gathered in Capitola like flies on raw meat, even in the winter months.

We slipped on our flip-flops and rolled up our pant legs as we sat in the Jeep enjoying the ocean view. Solow woke up and stretched. I hooked a leash onto his collar and we walked him down to the water. He let the bubbly surf wash over his feet as he kept an eye on a couple seagulls fighting over a dead fish a few yards ahead. He led us down the beach on all four bouncy legs, ignoring the wimpy waves, pulling us along under a bridge and onto a path that happened to lead to the apartments where Jake lived.

"Josie, do you know where you're going?"

"I've been here before, but today I'm just following Solow. It's not everyday he gets to go to the beach." Up ahead, I saw someone sitting in a deck chair in front of Jake's apartment. A closer look confirmed it was Jake working on his tan. An even closer look revealed a black eye that sunglasses didn't quite cover and a bruised chin.

"Hey, Jake." I waved to him.

He stood up and quickly slipped inside his apartment.

"It's me, Josephine," I shouted.

The screen door slammed behind him.

I peeked through the screen. "What's going on, Jake?"

"G'day, Josephine. I'm not feeling well today…."

I pushed the door open and walked in. "Is there something I can do to help?"

David followed me inside.

Solow growled.

"It's okay, Solow…."

Jake twirled around in his desk chair, automatically holding a hand out for Solow to sniff. "Your bloody feral friend came back," he said quietly, smoothing Solow's long velvety ears.

"What friend?" I scratched my head.

"Yeah, what friend?" David echoed.

"Kirby Levitt."

David frowned, obviously puzzled at the sound of his friend's name.

"Kirby, Kirby, Kirby…." Jake's bird repeated in a perfect Aussie accent.

"He brought the phone back, wanted me to look into it. I was sittin' right here in this chair when the bloke busted in, full a bull dust. Reckon he'd had too much neck oil, he did."

"What did you do?" I asked.

Jake removed his sunglasses. "I told the old piece a rubbish he was a thief and to get out. When I tried to stand up, he clocked me."

"That's awful, Jake. I'm so sorry it's come to this." I glanced at the blank look on David's face, realizing I had a lot of explaining to do to bring him up to speed.

"Do you still have the phone?" I asked Jake.

"I have it, but that cocky dag won't hear from me. I won't tell him a thing, but I'll let you know if I find anything else, Josephine."

"The phone numbers you gave me belonged to people who knew Mary. It's definitely the right phone, and the right place to look for pictures and information." Suddenly it occurred to me the phone might have belonged to Mary. Too bad the red cover was missing.

A smile crept across Jake's lips for the first time since we entered his apartment.

"Good on ya, Josephine. We need to find the bloody killer. I bet it's that loose cannon Kirby bloke of yours." Jake turned to face his desk, reached into a drawer and pulled out a small box containing a familiar-looking disassembled smart phone. He had already forgotten that we were in the room. David, Solow and I slipped outside. I quietly closed the screen door behind us. We walked the river path back to Capitola Beach where a mighty fog bank had already swallowed the sun in its relentless push eastward.

We ordered fish tacos at out favorite lunch place and ate them at a table on the deck facing an ocean smothered in fog. Being female, I shivered now and then but the guys had no problem with the chilly air. David noticed my shivers and offered to walk a couple blocks to fetch jackets from the Jeep. I smiled and wished him a safe journey.

"Is that you, Josephine?" a familiar female voice interrupted the eerily quiet fog-a-sphere.

I turned my head.

Solow slept contentedly, his body draped over my feet.

"Hi, Claudia…oh, hi, Buzz…."

"Who's the handsome fella?" she asked, as David arrived with the jackets and helped me into mine.

"David, I'd like you to meet my friends from Kati's watercolor class—Claudia and Buzz." I wondered why they were together. Last I'd heard they'd broken up and Claudia and Vick had looked pretty close. Yikes, more *Peyton Place*.

My honey stepped over to the next table, shook hands with the older couple and came back to finish off his tacos. Claudia's thick glasses followed him, along with the eyes of several women eating lunch at tables on the deck. My heart went from zero to sixty in one second when I realized for the millionth time how lucky I was.

Without an invitation, I hustled David and Solow over to Claudia's table. Buzz thought it was a great idea and helped us finish off our sweet potato fries. Claudia was a little more reserved, waiting until dessert to join the food fest. She left half her burger, preferring the mud pie David ordered for the four of us.

"Isn't this a lovely day?" she cooed, twirling a strand of yellow hair with her chubby fingers.

"If you like fog," Buzz grumped, staring at me with his one eye. "I ran into Kirby the other day. He seems to think you were involved in Mary's murder."

"Really," I said. "Actually, he's at the top of my short list of suspects. I'm sure he would love to hang it on me." I glanced at David to see his reaction. But knowing him, he would never get involved with gossip.

"Nice to meet you folks," David said as he stood and helped me out of my seat.

"Watch out for Kirby," I said to Buzz. "He doesn't have both oars in the water, if you know what I mean." I led Solow through the maze of tables, pulling him along as he stopped for every scrap of food that hit the deck. We finally made it back to the Jeep and David lifted my buddy into the back seat.

On our way home we motored through several different climates. Capitola and Aptos were immersed in fog while Watsonville enjoyed full sun and Aromas was experiencing sun with wisps of fog blowing in from the west. David dropped me and Solow at my house, saying he had a few chores to do but he would be back for a session of tree-trimming.

The tri-tip roast was thawed so I rubbed it with salt and herbs, plopped it in a baking dish and shoved it in the oven. I took laundry from the washing machine and tossed it in the dryer, popped a batch of popcorn and stirred up some hot chocolate. Painting would have to wait for another day. After a day of domestic chores, I would fain exhaustion and go to bed early, neglecting to tell David my plan to revisit Marla's neighborhood for another stakeout.

Chapter 17

Saturday evening was dedicated to performing my annual Christmas chores. Myrtle had miraculously survived thanks to an occasional drink of water from David. Like her namesake, she had a few brown spots but not enough to worry about. I trimmed the ends of several branches with scissors and inched her into a corner of the living room where she wouldn't have to deal with hot air from the free-standing wood-burning stove that usually created enough heat for ten large homes.

David arrived at the back door carrying a plastic bag bearing the "Dollar Store" logo, loaded with Christmas decorations. The first item he pulled out was an authentic plastic reproduction of mistletoe made in China. He held it over my head and planted a kiss on my lips. The plastic worked very well, every bit as well as the real greenery.

I hauled out a big plastic storage box from the loft and dragged it down the stairs. Unlike David's Dollar Store treasures, everything in the box was at least thirty years old, most items were much older thanks to my Grandmother. There were glass bird ornaments wrapped in tissue paper, tiny stuffed Santas, hand-painted glass balls and a large collection of Mickey and Minnie ornaments, my favorite characters from childhood.

I stepped back from the tree and almost stumbled over Solow who had found the perfect napping place on the rug. David tested two long strings of lights, but their glory was not to be. We decided a tree without lights would be beautifully old fashioned.

Not wishing to disturb my precious dog, I pushed in close to Myrtle's branches and David handed ornaments to me as he leaned over Solow's languid body. When the last ornament was hung, my silly dog woke up, sniffed the air and loped into the kitchen to see if the roast was done.

"He'd make a great chef," David laughed.

"He can have the job if he wants it," I said, as I lifted the roasting pan from the oven and set it on the counter. To my surprise, the meat, potatoes and roasted vegetables were perfectly done. David tossed the salad while I lit two candles and turned down the lights.

David put on some old Christmas music and opened the dining room drapes so that we could look at the full moon.

"You have company, Josie."

"What? Oh, it's Mel, Mary's brother…the guy who fixed my roof…."

David grinned. "And fell off. I see he's still wearing a boot. Must have been quite a fall."

"I'll get the door," I said, switching on lights as I went.

Solow barked at the front door and wagged his tail when Mel entered the room.

"Wow, smells good in here," he said, glancing at the dinning room table.

"Hi, Mel; do you know David?"

"Now I do. Nice to meet ya, pal." They shook hands. "Looks like you two have plans….I tried all day to get you on the phone. I just wanted to discuss a certain auto-theft."

I glanced across the room. Sure enough, the answering machine's red light was blinking.

"Don't mind me," David said, "I'll be in the kitchen opening the wine." He left the living room, but in my modest little house, the living room, dining room and kitchen were all open to each other.

"What's going on?" I whispered.

"I'm going out of town and won't be back until tomorrow. I hope you don't decide to do a stakeout tonight without me around."

"You're right. I'll probably just stay home tonight."

"With him?"

"Of course, we're decorating for Christmas," I said, taking in the spicy cologne the man had liberally splashed on himself.

"Sweet. Guess I'll be off. I'm on my way to Big Sur," Mel announced in a voice strong enough to cross three or more rooms. "Nice meetin' ya, David."

The front door closed, a truck door slammed and gravel hit the porch.

Like civilized people, David and I turned down the lights, filled our plates and clinked our glasses.

"Here's to Myrtle," I raised my glass.

"Here's to us," he said.

"Here's to your family."

"And to yours....and what auto-theft?"

"Didn't I tell you? Marla's car was stolen last night, but the thief brought it back...."

"I think the wine is getting to you," he laughed.

I laughed. Thank goodness that was the end of that conversation. We watched one of our favorite Christmas movies, and then the ten o'clock news came on. The reporter talked about a new rehabilitation program at the Dominican Hospital in Santa Cruz. I wondered if Mr. Herrera had ever tried to be rehabilitated, or if he was unfixable. I made a mental note to talk to Marla about it.

David yawned. "Josie, honey, I have to go home now. I have an early morning dental appointment and I need time to worry about it."

"You'll be fine. Worrying isn't going to help," I yawned. We kissed and said goodnight. David walked home with his flashlight and I prepared a thermos of coffee and bagged up a roast beef sandwich. In order to concentrate on Marla's car, I decided to leave the CF Carter mystery novel at home tonight.

Before I left the house, I closed the drapes, noticing that the moon and stars had disappeared behind clouds. After two trips to the truck with a cold wind blowing hair into my eyes, I finally had all my stake-out supplies stashed behind the front seats and Solow in the passenger seat. I fired up the truck, feeling like the cab was my home away from home. I had always enjoyed driving, but the gas stations were killing me.

As Solow and I motored across the Watsonville valley floor, better known as the "Salad Bowl of the World," I sang along with Christmas carols on the radio and Solow woofed and howled his approval. Already it was a night to remember. I hadn't burned any part of our dinner and Myrtle had survived all of my neglect—she looked radiantly happy to be decorated. Mel would be in Big Sur and out of my way at the stake-out and the moon was in hiding thanks to some friendly clouds.

"We're here, old buddy." I curbed the truck across the street and half a block down from Marla's house. I checked my watch. It was eleven-fifteen. Marla's porch light was on, along with one light at Ricky's house and a few other lights up and down the block. At first, I stared at Marla's white SUV constantly, but as time slowly ticked by I caught myself drifting off. My chin hit my chest and instantly I was awake again. I took a few sips of lukewarm coffee, practiced my Spanish on Solow and then the chin hit the chest.

I checked my watch about every three minutes. At twelve-ten, a bicycle rider passed under a streetlight two blocks away, and swerved into Marla's driveway. Even though I'd never seen the woman in person, I knew for sure it was Juanita when she dismounted, opened the side gate and disappeared behind the house. Who else would be riding a bike at midnight? I knew she worked the night shift and tried to imagine what it would be like to live in a garage and work at night.

For the tenth time, I wished I'd brought my book.

Solow did a couple woof, woof sounds as he awkwardly circled the bucket seat with his long body.

"Gotta go, little buddy?" I hadn't remembered to bring a leash, but there was no one in sight so I rounded the truck and helped Solow down to the sidewalk. The instant his fourth paw hit concrete, he was running at top basset speed chasing a flash of yellow fur that turned out to be a very athletic cat. My whispered pleas for him to come back fell on over-sized deaf ears.

I was just about to climb back into the truck to get warm when a streak of yellow zipped past my legs, careened to the right and crossed the street with Solow just a few feet behind. They disappeared through a hedge that ran front to back between Marla's house and Ricky's mom's house.

"Meow..me..ow..me..yow!" screamed the cat.

"Woof, woof, woof." Then a long howl.

"Meyow..eeow!"

A light went on at Ricky's house.

I quickly climbed into the truck and slouched down in my seat. Should I try to rescue Solow or keep my undercover status? Suddenly the interior of my truck seemed light. But the light was not from headlights coming down the street. Those traitorous clouds had blown away, exposing a big old moon. Everything in the neighborhood was easy to see, including my truck.

I held my breath, raised my head and peeked out the window.

Ricky's porch light flickered on, the door opened and Ricky stood on the porch in his boxer shorts. His gaze immediately went to my truck.

I raised up for a second and peeked out the window.

Ricky's lanky white boxered-frame crossed the street at an angle, obviously aiming for my Mazda.

I curled into a ball with my head on the passenger seat, shivering at the thought of his being mostly naked on such a cold night.

"Tap, tap."

I sat up. There was Ricky, smiling, his head cocked to one side.

I rolled down the window. "Ricky. You're up late." I shivered as cold air blew across my face.

"Guess we both are. Was that your dog I heard?"

"Could be. I was visiting Marla when Solow ran away. I've been looking for him all night." I fixed my face into a tired, hopeless, disgusted expression.

"Like, I'm a light sleeper," Ricky said, ruffling his semi-short curly hair with both hands. "I like to make sure nothing bad happens on this street, you know, like burglaries and that sort of thing. Like, I hope you find your dog, Josephine. Good night." He turned and walked carefully back to his home on bare feet.

I settled into my seat and waited for Solow to come back. He always obeyed me except when a cat was involved. My chin hit my chest and the next thing I knew, on-coming headlights lit up the cab. I blinked my eyes and yawned. It was one o'clock in the morning. A small car pulled to the curb behind Marla's SUV and two people got out. I watched them walk up to the front door. Their words were muffled by the wind so I rolled the window down, but the wind was so cold that I quickly rolled it up again.

Obviously, a discussion was in full swing on the Milford porch. Minutes ticked by. Finally, the guy wearing a trench coat marched out to the little car at the curb, climbed in and slammed the door. The car took off with a squeal and a roar. As it whizzed by my truck, I recognized Mary's classic Porsche driven by its new owner, Kirby.

When Marla finally turned off her porch light, I climbed out of the truck, flashlight in hand, to look for Solow. Starting with the hedge and ending with a crawlspace under Ricky's house, I finally found my filthy dirty pal stuck between a pile of bricks and a short stack of rotting two-by-fours. His collar was caught on a roll of chicken wire and he seemed very confused about the whole situation. He whimpered as I untangled the wire, pushed a few bricks aside and pulled him out of the space by his collar, still on my knees and cringing at the thought of spiders.

"Like, what happened?" a familiar young male voice asked.

I stood up and turned around. "Ricky. What are you doing…?"

"What am I doing? Really?"

"You don't have to be sarcastic. Solow chased a cat under your house and why do you have all that junk under there anyway?"

"Now who's being sarcastic?" he said, hands on hips, boxers bright white in the moonlight.

"If I was your mother I'd tell you to get back in the house. It's freezing in this wind."

"If you were my mother I'd have you committed," he muttered.

I walked Solow back to the truck.

Ricky's front door slammed.

Marla's door snapped shut.

Chapter 18

Sunday morning I promised myself I'd complete at least one painting before the end of the day because the end of the day was when I was expected at Mom and Dad's for dinner. After breakfast, I tidied up the house, admiring Ms. Myrtle and all the other Christmas decorations as I vacuumed a couple rooms and emptied the wastebaskets. Christmas carols streamed from my old boom box and Solow wore his red and green plaid holiday collar. Every time he scratched himself or ran through the house, two little bells tinkled.

When my chores had been completed, I had to face the toughest work of all, painting a picture suitable for framing. I thumbed through a large basket of old greeting cards and postcards I'd saved over the years. Nothing looked interesting so I moved on to my collection of old calendars. One photograph caught my attention—the silhouette of a lone duck creating a wake across silent silver water. The scene included reeds, trees in the distance and a moon reflected on the water.

When my paper was taped to the board—paints and water ready—the phone rang. I was tempted to not answer, but what if it was Mom or Dad needing help? On second thought, that was not likely because my folks were very independent. But I decided to answer the phone anyway, just in case.

"Josephine, it's me, Buzz. Just checking up on your order—you know, for frames."

"Hi, Buzz. I'm not sure yet how many I need. By the end of the day I hope to have eight paintings and a possible thirteen by the end of the week."

"I'll put together eight frames with mats. Don't want to wait to the last minute."

"Thanks, Buzz, for looking out for me."

"Have you seen Marla lately?" he asked.

"Um, not much…."

"What does that mean? Either ya saw her or ya didn't," he said, sounding a bit snarky.

I thought about how much I should tell him. Did he know that his friend, Kirby was dating Marla? At least, that was how it looked in the wee hours of the morning. Was Buzz chasing after Marla too? I didn't want to get involved.

"Sorry, Josephine, I'm feeling like I got kicked to the curb. I think she's seeing someone else, but you don't need to be concerned."

"I'm sorry, Buzz. I don't know what to tell you…."

"Sorry I mentioned it. I'll work on the frames and you let me know the final count."

"I'll do that, Buzz. Thanks for calling." I rolled my eyes and hung up the phone. The old folks had way too much drama going on. Was Mary murdered because of a romance triangle? In her journal she talked about Buzz and Kirby. Maybe she wasn't able to juggle them well enough to keep herself out of trouble. Now it looked like Marla was juggling the same two guys.

After an hour of painting, I called Alicia.

"Allie, are you painting?"

"Not right now; I finished a painting of the lake half an hour ago. What are you doing?"

"I'm halfway into a new painting, but I can't help thinking about Mary and her life-style. It seems she had two guys after her. Maybe someone's temper flared and, well, you know."

"Jo, just paint, and don't get sidetracked. You know how you are."

"What do you mean by that?"

"You know how you are when there's a murder and you want to figure out who did it, you focus on that and nothing else," she said in her 'calm-down' mother-voice.

"I don't think that's necessarily true…."

"Jo."

"Okay, sometimes it's true. This case is driving me nuts and I'm not getting much sleep."

"Oh?"

"Mainly because I'm watching Marla's car at night. It was stolen the first night, but the crook brought it back…."

"Jo, go have a cup of coffee and keep your mind on painting. That's my best advice. Bye."

Turning back to my painting, I realized I'd created a wonderful sky above a rather convincing body of water. I hoped to add the duck and foliage without ruining the picture. To calm my nerves, I decided to pop some popcorn and put on one of my favorite movies, *The Christmas Story.* I knew the thing by heart, but when the dogs ravaged a roasted turkey and Ralphie's Dad blew a gasket, I was holding my sides with laughter for the hundredth time.

Solow howled.

The phone rang.

I put the movie on hold and answered the phone.

"Hi, Josephine, it's Marla. I'm in your neighborhood. Would it be alright if I dropped in for a minute?"

"Of course, it would be fine. I'm just watching an old movie…I hear a car…."

"I'm in your driveway; bye."

The doorbell rang. I opened the door for my disheveled friend.

"What's going on, Marla? Come sit down over here on the couch."

"Thank you, Josephine. I'm so confused." She plopped down onto the couch, straightening her hair with her fingers. "I was all set to go to church this morning, but my car wouldn't start and Mel wasn't home so I asked Ricky to look at it. The boy dragged himself out of bed looking like he'd been in a fight with a hungry bear. A little while later he knocked on the door and told me the car was fixed so I paid him the usual forty dollars."

"At minimum wage, that would be four hours pay," I quipped.

"Half an hour or four hours, it was too much!" she scowled. "I decided to take down the camera Mel had installed above the porch and see if it caught anything suspicious."

My heart did a double thump. *Would I be in the video?*

"You can imagine my shock when I saw young Ricky, late at night, with his head under the hood of my car," Marla stammered indignantly.

"Is that all you saw?"

"Isn't that enough?" She crossed one leg over the other and fiddled with her bracelets. Solow moved from his favorite place by the window over to Marla's foot. I held my breath, but she seemed all right with Solow falling asleep on her foot.

"What do you think he was doing under the hood?" Even as I asked the question, I guessed the answer. Of course, he was un-doing something so the car wouldn't start, so he could later make some money fixing it. Mary must have been a victim of the same trick.

"Marla, does Ricky have a key to your car?"

"Well, yes; I gave him one a couple weeks ago so he could work on…oh my gosh, that's how he…."

"He had a nice little racket going," I said. "I wonder if he did the same thing to Mary."

"Of course he did. Several times her car wouldn't start and Ricky fixed it for her, that little rascal. What do you think I should do, Josephine?"

"I wouldn't call the cops or tell his mother if he promises to never do such a thing again. If he breaks his word, you have video proof." I didn't mention the possibility that Ricky borrowed her car for a joy ride one night because I hadn't seen who did it. Besides, it had been returned. "And be sure you get the key back."

Because the Ricky business was on her mind, Marla had forgotten to eat breakfast and was overdue for lunch. I invited her to have an impromptu lunch with me. I put together tuna and cheese sandwiches, a green salad and two mugs of hot tea.

"Josephine, this is so sweet of you," Marla said as she tossed a piece of crust to Solow and laughed when he caught it with his mouth. "He's really a very sweet dog."

"He is, isn't he?" I smiled, glad she finally realized what a sweetheart he was. "Now I have a question for you, Marla. As you know, I read parts of Mary's journal—actually, a whole year's worth, and the thing I gleaned from it was her relationships with Kirby and Buzz. I'm wondering if the romantic triangle caused…."

"Josephine, you're on the wrong track. Kirby and Mary were friends and lovers for over forty years—since they were teenagers. Buzz's wife died about five years ago and then he dated Claudia, but that didn't work out. Mary felt sorry for him and was just trying to be a friend. She wasn't interested in marrying anyone. She loved her freedom."

"Wow, there goes that theory." I rubbed my chin, hoping another idea would miraculously take its place.

"Don't take it so hard, Josephine. I still think Mary stepped too close to the edge and fell. You know how wibbly-wobbly she was. It's probably nobody's fault." She stood up to go. "Now I have to go and give Ricky both barrels. I'll let you know how he reacts to my lecture."

Hours later, I still hadn't shaken the feeling that Mary had been murdered. Fortunately, I was able to paint and think about other things at the same time. My mural painting career had given me lots of time to practice multi-tasking. As I recreated Ricky's money-racket in my head, my brush created a faint forest along the horizon, a lone duck skimming across the water and reeds growing at the water's edge, all silhouetted by the moon.

The lone duck made me think of Ricky, alone in his mother's house...the mother never around. Wait a minute! There was probably a girlfriend somewhere. He had a key for Marla's car. I wondered how many times he'd used the car. A Lexus SUV was pretty nice transportation for a young man without a job.

To celebrate the completion of my newest painting, I called David to ask him over early. The line was busy. I called Alicia—no one home. I called her cell number.

"Hi, Allie; where are you?"

"We're watching Trigger's soccer game, freezing our backsides into popsicles. What's up?"

"Not much...just getting ready to go to Mom and Dad's for dinner. Call me tomorrow."

"Okay, Jo, tell the folks hi."

I thought about calling Mom, but she'd be flying around her kitchen putting together her idea of a traditional Christmas meal. She would try her hand at making plum pudding again, which is actually made out of raisins and dried fruit. It was all about tradition, which was very strange coming from my non-traditional mother. She would ask Dad for help lifting the turkey into the oven. She would over-cook the Brussels sprouts while he added extra ingredients to the eggnog. Every year we had an intimate, traditional family get-together before Christmas there because the big party blow-out was always at my house.

I tried David's number again.

"Hi, Josie. I'll be over in half an hour to pick you up."

"I don't remember asking you to Mom and Dad's Christmas dinner. How is it that you never forget anything and I forget so many things? It's like, I turned fifty and instantly my mind is mush. I don't think that happens to men."

"Other things happen, believe me. See ya soon, sweetie."

Half an hour later, I was dressed in my white silk blouse and long skirt. I slipped into silver four-inch heels to go with my silver earrings and bracelets. David arrived wearing charcoal slacks and a baby blue sweater—yum. *White Christmas* played in the background as he walked in the door. I held up the fake sprig of mistletoe and we kissed. Kisses were always better when we were dressed up.

"Hey, did you paint that?" he asked, pointing to the lone duck picture still taped to a board.

"Sure did." I smiled proudly.

"That's funny. I have that same picture on last year's calendar…."

"We should be going." I took his arm and led him out to the Jeep. Solow followed, tail wagging. I climbed into the passenger seat while David helped Solow into the backseat. "Do you mind if we stop in Capitola? Marla left her umbrella here."

"No problem," he said as he turned the Jeep toward Watsonville. "Beautiful night, don't you think?"

"Yes, it is. Ooh, I saw a shooting star!"

Twenty-five minutes later, we arrived at Marla's house. All the lights were on. I rang the doorbell and Marla opened the door, a big smile on her face and chocolate frosting smeared on her apron. Christmas music played as we followed her into the kitchen where Laurita stood on a chair pushed up to the counter. Instead of an apron, a tea towel was tied around her tiny waist. Powdered sugar and chocolate smears had found their way onto her hair, her nose, the towel and even one shoe. She looked up and laughed.

Marla pulled a cookie sheet out of the oven and set it aside to cool.

"Oh, you dear thing, you brought back my umbrella," she cooed.

"Umbella," Laurita mimicked.

Something caught my eye outside on the patio. It was Juanita, riding away on her bike. She had lots of black wavy hair flowing from a knitted cap, but so far I'd never seen her face.

"How's everything going?" I asked Marla.

"Just making Christmas cookies…oh, you mean…just fine, thank you. Ricky said he was sorry."

"Good!" David and I excused ourselves and let the bakers get back to their baking. The smell of warm cookies had put me in the mood for what turned out to be an interesting pre-Christmas dinner. Interesting because Mom said she thought she might be gluten intolerant and she'd eliminated wheat flour from her gravy recipe, rolls, pies, pudding and cookies. She had substituted rice flour, thinking we wouldn't notice the difference.

Myrtle, Mom and Dad's friend from next door, relaxed by the fireplace while my parents worked at making gravy, carving the turkey, mashing potatoes and tossing the salad. A plate of cookies sat on the coffee table in front of Myrtle's seat on the couch. She chewed on one little cookie for quite some time, but finally set it down and left it. I took it as a warning.

I offered to help in the kitchen, but Mom said everything was under control so I went back to the living room to sit with Myrtle and David. Just as I nestled close to David, Dad came to him. He needed someone to mash the potatoes while he carved the turkey.

David left, I reached for a cookie.

Myrtle shook her head, giving me a stern look.

"Not so good?" I asked, setting the cookie back on the plate.

She shook her head again. "Not unless you like sandstone."

"Mom told me she went off wheat. Maybe it's not as easy as it sounds." I wasn't completely surprised since some of her friends were on gluten-free diets. Naturally, she would want to do the same.

Mom and I were quite opposite. She liked trendy stuff and sometimes was a trend-setter herself. She liked the newest popular wall color, had to have a certain brand of tennis racket and followed the latest trend in shoes and purses. But she was smart, packing away her skinny jeans for a few years until they became popular again. Her big, big purse was in storage, temporarily replaced with a mini-purse until the big ones came back in style again.

On the other hand, Dad was an old-fashioned guy—loved his Bing Crosby Christmas carol collection, his fifty-year-old golf clubs and every goofy pin on his old fishing hat.

I understood my father's sentimentality and admired Mom's social aptitude, but I didn't understand how a cookie could taste like chocolate-covered sand.

Chapter 18

Monday morning I received an urgent call from Claudia. She wanted to meet me in Capitola—as if I hadn't already made a million trips to the little beach town. I told Claudia I'd meet her at the cliff where Mary had painted her last painting. Despite traffic and windy weather, I arrived at the cliff's public parking at 9:50, ten minutes early. I decided to walk down to the lower path and check out the infamous bench. I zipped up my jacket and adjusted my knitted scarf as I walked. I seemed to be the only person around.

"Ooga, ooga!"

I stepped to my right just in time. A bicyclist came up from behind and flew by me without slowing down.

"Oh my God!" I said to myself, as all the blood in my brain drained into my frozen-to-the-ground feet. I stood still, slack-jawed, unable to move. Someone from behind tapped my shoulder. I spun around ready to defend myself, but it was only Claudia.

"Josephine, I'm sorry I scared you. Are you all right?" she said as she took my arm and led me down the path ten feet to the bench.

We sat down and I shivered.

"Something's wrong, am I right?" Claudia asked.

I was so busy trying to remember every detail of the bike and it's rider that I forgot to answer her question.

"Josephine…."

"Sorry, Claudia, I just saw the same bike that I saw the day Mary was killed. Same *ooga*, same black sweats, same blue backpack. How's your ankle?"

"It's pretty good...."

"Good, let's walk." I stood and began walking in the westerly direction the bike had taken, at a quick pace. Claudia half walked, half ran to catch up. We kept up the pace for about fifteen minutes as the path took us westward around the point, then north along Opal Cliff Drive. We passed 49th Street, the street we would have taken if we were going to Marla's house on Jade Street. We hurried along Portola Drive for another ten blocks.

I stopped to catch my breath and noticed Claudia was two blocks behind me, bent over, gasping for air. I sat on the sidewalk waiting for her to catch up.

"I'm sorry...Josephine, but I'm not...built for racing." She sucked in buckets of air as she plopped down beside me.

"I wish I could catch up to the biker and see who it is," I said. "I want to ask if the person saw anything suspicious the day of the murder."

"That's what...this is all about?" Claudia gasped and wrinkled her nose, rolling her eyes behind huge magnification. I wanted...to meet you today...because I know something...."

"About Mary's murder?"

"Yes, I just need to...get my breathing...under control." We were both bushed so we sat another five minutes before getting back to the Mary-subject. Just as Claudia opened her mouth to talk, a city bus pulled up to the curb. It stopped two feet from where we sat, close enough to feel motor-heat on our faces. We quickly stood up and began walking back toward the Capitola cliffs and Mary's bench.

"Did you notice the curb was painted yellow?" I asked Claudia.

She didn't answer.

I looked back over my shoulder. She was hobbling along two blocks behind me. I stopped to wait for her but she was taking so long, I decided to double back.

"Oh, Josephine, I can't go on." She lifted her pant leg. The ankle was obviously swollen.

"Euw, that looks painful. Tell you what, I'll go back and get my truck and meet you right here in front of this tattoo parlor. Just sit on the edge of this planter box over here. I won't be long." I helped Claudia over to a long concrete planter box full of African daisies mingling with milkweed and crab grass, gave her a reassuring pat on the shoulder, turned and walked swiftly away.

The return trip was slow-going and exhausting. I leaned into the wind, pushing myself to keep going forward. Half-way to the truck, the sky darkened and suddenly opened up, dumping hail on everything. The little icy balls bounced all over the sidewalk, making the concrete slippery and my progress that much slower.

My emotions had run amuck. Besides being cold and wet, I was mad at myself for not finding the bike rider and sad for Claudia who was hurting and probably as wet and cold as I was, but most of all, I was anxious to hear the information Claudia wanted to give me.

When I finally completed my return trip back to the tattoo parlor on Portola Drive, the planter box was empty. Claudia was nowhere in sight. I drove about five blocks north, ten blocks south and all around the jewel neighborhood, finally stopping at Marla's house. Marla said she had Claudia's phone number in her little book and went to the kitchen to find it. She came back with the number written on the back of a business card. I turned the card over.

"Victor Smathers Used Cars?" I read out loud.

"Yes." Marla smiled. "He has given us some very good deals over the years."

"The blue Porsche?"

She nodded. "Mary bought it about ten years ago when Vick was still in the business. Kirby had his eye on it, but she was quicker."

"You know Claudia Berton from book club and painting class, but have you known her long?" I asked.

Marla chuckled. "We all grew up in the Santa Cruz and Capitola area, including Claudia. We went to school together, the boys went off to war, a couple of them didn't come home including the one Mary was engaged to. After that, she said phooey on marriage. She seemed happy to be single. I have a daughter, but her father didn't come home from the war."

"Excuse me, Marla, I really should call Claudia to see if she's okay." I punched the number into my cell phone and waited. An exhausted voice said, "Heh-lo."

"Claudia? Are you okay?"

"Is this Josephine?"

"Yes, I'm calling to find out what happened to you…."

"I took the bus home," she said matter-of-factly.

"Okay, any chance I can come over…."

"I'm going to rest for a couple hours. I might need to go to the doctor."

"I'll be over in two hours and if you decide to go to the doctor, I'll take you." She didn't say no so I hung up. I asked Marla for Claudia's address and jotted it down on Kirby's business card. It was almost noon and I was hungry so I asked Marla if she'd like to go somewhere for lunch. She said she had homemade turkey soup in her fridge.

Laurita knocked on the back door and Marla let her in. Still wearing pajamas, the little girl stayed for lunch, adding giggles and squeals to our turkey soup experience. Marla helped Laurita place a napkin on her lap and gently corrected her when she made slurping noises with her soup.

Marla smiled and said, "I feel like I finally have a granddaughter."

"You two are a perfect fit," I said. "Please pass the salt. Thank you, Laurita." The little girl reported to Marla that Christmas was coming soon and Santa Claus would bring her a bicycle with training wheels. She finished her soup and asked to be excused because her kitty needed her.

Marla kissed the top of Laurita's head and shooed her out the door.

"As many times as I've been here," I said, "I've never met her parents."

"Juanita and Pedro really do exist, but they let me have Laurita most of the day so she can learn to speak English. I don't know why her mother doesn't teach her. Oh, well, I love having Laurita here. She's doing well, don't you think?"

"Sure is. I'm sorry to eat and run, but I need to take a look at Claudia's swollen ankle and see if she should go see a doctor." I pushed away from the table. "Thanks for lunch."

My little truck roared up Forty-First Avenue, turned right on Soquel Drive and left on Porter. A half mile out, I found Claudia's address—an old farm house, one of the few left in Soquel, which she shared with her elderly mother. The old lady answered the door and ushered me into the high-ceilinged living room where Claudia rested on the sofa, her leg propped up on two needlepoint pillows, a sack of frozen peas balanced on top of the afflicted ankle.

"Are you awake, Claudia?" I whispered.

She snorted twice, opened her eyes and reached for her glasses.

"Oh, it's you, Josephine."

"How's your ankle feeling…?"

"Better, I think. I guess I should tell you about my nephew, Trevor."

"I thought you had news about Mary's murder," I said.

"That's what it's about. You see, I saw my nephew recently and he told me he saw something while he was hang-gliding that day near the cliffs. He recognized me over by the parking lot, but I didn't see him. Trevor told me he saw a little girl holding either a phone or a camera while this older lady wearing a red sweater stood with her back to the cliff. He said he swung around the cliff area for a second look, but the lady was gone and the little girl was running down the path, already a few blocks away, heading toward Opal Cliff Drive."

"Good grief. I need to talk to Marla. Anything I can do for you before I leave?" I said, as I casually moved closer to the front door.

"Maybe you could move the peas a little more that way?" Claudia waved her hand at her foot."

Her mother didn't look up, just worked on her knitting from across the room.

Bending over the couch, I quickly rearranged the sack of peas for Claudia, advised her to get some rest and to call me if she needed a ride to the doctor—but not right away. The screen door slammed behind me as I ran across the old wooden porch and down three creaky steps. As I hurried along a winding garden path to the curb where my truck was parked, I thought about the hang glider I'd seen the day Mary died.

My truck jerked to a stop behind Marla's SUV in front of her house. I jumped out and ran to the front door. It was locked. I pushed on the doorbell over and over. Finally I walked around the house to the patio in the back. A gust of wind blew damp hair across my face, reminding me again of that fateful day at the cliffs.

After knocking on the back door, I heard foot steps behind me and twirled around, pulling hair out of my eyes.

"Josephine, was that you sitting on the doorbell?" Mel asked. His lips curled into a smile as he looked over my windswept appearance.

"Yep, I need to talk to Marla right away."

"Sounds important. She took Laurita for a walk to the store. Can I help you?" he asked, looking ruggedly under-dressed in his Levis and t-shirt. Wind whistled around the corner of the house, and clouds covered the sun. "Let's go inside; you look frozen."

"I got caught in a hail storm today and I'm still not dry." We stepped into Marla's kitchen and sat down at the table. "Mel, what do you think of the Herreras? Are they good parents?"

"I never thought about it before." He rubbed the stubble on his chin. "The mom works a lot and sleeps during the day, and Mr. Herrera hardly ever comes outside. He's only in his twenties, but doesn't look well sittin' around in a wheelchair all the time."

"If it wasn't for Marla, the little girl wouldn't have much of a life," I said.

"And Mary before Marla," he added. I didn't understand it at first, but I get it now. The little kid needs someone to take care of her. So answering your question…no, the Herreras are not very good parents."

"The thing I don't understand is why hasn't Marla reported the parents? She's a social worker…."

"Yeah," Mel said, "she *was* a social worker and she knows what would happen. She would feel terrible if the family was ripped apart. The way it is now, she makes sure Laurita has everything she needs. And now that she's quit her job, she has plenty of time."

"I didn't know she quit—good for her. I knew she was ready to retire."

"Josephine, can I get you something to drink…?"

We heard the front door open. Marla and Laurita clambered into the kitchen talking and laughing. The little girl stopped to give Mel a hug. She started to take her jacket off but Marla told her to keep it on and go outside to feed her cat. Mel accompanied her out the back door.

Marla fluttered around the kitchen offering me food and drink, commenting on Laurita's good humor and Mel's helpfulness. Finally, she flopped into a chair and asked why I looked so worried.

"I just came from Claudia's," I said. "It seems her nephew was hang gliding along the cliffs the day Mary died."

A huge silence took over the kitchen. Each tick-tock from the wall clock sounded like a metal drumstick hitting a fifty gallon metal drum. Marla's tea kettle suddenly hissed, unseating both of us. We looked at each other, laughed and sat down again.

"Where were you the day your sister fell into the ocean?" I asked.

"I had a headache that morning. I slept late and then Juanita asked me to watch Laurita for awhile…."

"That's all you did?"

"Not exactly. Laurita wanted to know where Mary was so I thought we would walk down to the ocean and see how the painting was going. I bundled her up and we walked all the way to Mary's bench. The wind was so cold, I just wanted to go home, but Laurita wanted to stay with Mary."

"Did you tell the police all of this?"

"No, because they didn't ask me. Anyway, I had my phone with me so I took a picture of Mary's painting. It was lovely. She was an excellent painter."

"Then what happened?" My heart was racing.

"Laurita wanted to take a picture of Mary so Mary took her phone out of her pocket, handed it to Laurita and the little sweetheart clicked off a whole bunch of pictures, even some with Mary standing with her back to the cliff. I wasn't worried. I didn't think she was too close to the edge."

"What happened next?" I whispered, as my throat dried up.

"Nothing. I said goodbye to Mary." Marla looked at the ceiling trying to remember everything. "I turned away and started walking home. Laurita was being a bit stubborn about leaving, but a minute later she caught up to me…she loves to run. That's all I know."

"Do you remember seeing anyone else on the path?"

"I don't remember seeing anyone…but my memory isn't what it used to be," she sighed.

One fact hit me square in my heart. Sweet little Laurita was the last person to be with Mary, an unspeakable fact that we all would have to live with.

Chapter 19

Tuesday's painting turned out pretty well if you like old barns and such. Half a mile down the road from my house stood a sway-backed barn and a mostly peeled three-story pump house. A vacant, falling down farm house stood an acre away, looking like no one had lived in it in the last fifty years. Talk about a perfect picture! But Tuesday's weather forecast didn't inspire outdoor projects. I knew that even the lightest sprinkle of rain would ruin a watercolor painting in seconds.

I parked my truck at the side of the road, turned the radio to a station with Christmas music and painted the scene from inside the cab. My Mazda's interior was as cozy as a tiny windowed closet. I pushed the seat back as far as it would go and tried to forget that I had no elbow room. Fortunately, the green grass, rustic buildings and stormy cloud pattern were inspiring. Things went pretty well if you discount accidentally dipping my brush into the coffee mug instead of the water jar. After a couple hours of painting, the liquids looked quite a bit alike.

When my picture was eighty percent finished and my feet were ninety percent frozen, I closed up my paint box, pulled the front seat forward and turned the key.

"Urr, urr, urr," and silence. Even the radio had gone silent. I knocked my knee on the steering wheel as I stamped the floor with one cold foot. I pulled my cell phone out of my purse and punched in my auto insurance number from a faded peeling sticker on the windshield. A recording said my call was very much appreciated and to stay on the line another fifty-two minutes until a professional could talk to me. I heard a click and then some very irritating music.

No way would I put up with such bad service, not to mention bad music. I punched in David's number.

"Hey, Josie, what's up?"

"My truck won't start...."

"Can't help you right now, sweetie, I'm in the dentist's chair and she just walked into the room."

I heard a female voice—the smooth, flawless voice I remembered.

The dentist said something to David before we hung up. I had nothing against the dentist except that I'd already met her at a party and she was a gorgeous blond. But I trusted David to know the difference between true friendship and blond blindness.

My second choice was Mel. He answered on the second ring. I explained my predicament and he promised to meet me at my house within the hour. I locked the truck doors and trudged home. Solow looked surprised to see me. After all, I'd left in the truck and came home without it.

By the time Mel arrived, I had a chicken salad and tomato soup lunch waiting for him. He had coffee with his gingerbread cookie, I had tea and Solow licked crumbs off the floor.

"Josephine, has Marla or anyone told you about Laurita?" Something in Mel's voice sent shivers down my spine.

"What about her?"

"Marla said she knocked on Mr. Herrera's door this morning, looking for Laurita. He came to the door, eyes all red and everything. Said his wife and little girl were on their way to Mexico."

"What are you saying?" I stammered.

"Like I said, they're on their way to Tijuana where the grandmother lives."

"But why?"

"Yesterday, Marla told Juanita what happened the day my sister died, you know, that Laurita was the last person to see Mary. She got all weird, afraid the police would come and get her daughter."

"No one is accusing Laurita of anything…."

"Yeah, but Juanita was scared stiff. She called a taxi this morning and Mr. Herrera thinks they caught the train…."

"The poor man, he can't even chase after them," I said as I cleared the table.

"He wanted me to go bring them back. How would I do that?" Mel laughed.

Mel drove me to the farm, did a U-turn and parked nose-to-nose with my Mazda. I sat in his truck as he pulled jumper cables out of the back of the pickup, popped the hood of my truck and attached the cables to both vehicles. I climbed into my truck while Mel jumped into his driver's seat and started his engine. I turned my key and my engine responded with a healthy roar.

I waved to Mel as he turned his truck around and headed for home.

The Mazda idled a few minutes before I took it for a long ride to recharge the battery. As usual, Capitola was my destination. I parked in front of Marla's house. Her SUV and Mel's truck were missing. I walked to the back of the house and knocked on Mr. Herrera's door. There was movement behind the door and finally it opened.

"Olah." Red-rimmed eyes blinked and looked up at me. The handsome young Latino father backed up his wheelchair into a small but well organized living room/kitchen combination.

I stepped into his apartment. "Mr. Herrera, my name is Josephine. Is it true that your esposa and hija are going to Mexico?"

He took a moment to dissect my words, nodded, and dropped his head to his chest.

"How can I help you?" I asked.

Mr. Herrera listened carefully, trying to make sense of my English. "Por favor, find mi nina…mi Laurita." He wiped tears from both eyes.

A huge lump had already lodged itself in my throat. My eyes stung. "We should call the police for help…."

"No!" his voice boomed. "No can call…problema grande."

"But, sir, you can trust the police in this country…."

"No!" He put his palms together and pleaded. "Por favor, no call."

"Okay, I won't call. I'll find her," I promised, not having a clue how to do it. But a promise is a promise. Somehow I would have to find Laurita and her mother and bring them back.

Laurita's kitty cowered in the corner of the room.

Mr. Herrera rolled over to a small kitchen table, picked up a hand-written note and handed it to me. It was written in Spanish, but I recognized several words in it like *autobus*, *tren*, *San Louis Obispo, San Diego* and *Tijuana.* Obviously, Juanita planned to take a bus to San Louis Obispo and the train to San Diego and somehow cross the border into TJ where the grandma lived.

I handed Mr. Herrera a piece of scrap paper and one of Laurita's crayons and asked the man to write down Juanita's mother's address in Tijuana and a phone number before I left.

Stepping outside, I felt a slap of reality as gusts of cold air brushed my cheeks and played with Marla's wind chimes hanging from the eves. The screen door banged against the back door and Laurita's plastic puppy skittered across the patio. What was I to do? I had made a promise I probably couldn't keep, but I had to try. If Claudia hadn't told me about her nephew seeing the little girl with Mary, and I hadn't told Marla, who then told Juanita, none of this would have happened. I felt guilty, sorry and sad. I had to do something.

When I circled the house and was about to climb into my truck, Marla pulled up at the curb and cut the engine. She ran up to me and grabbed my arm.

"Josephine, I need your help…."

"I think I know the problem." I held up Mr. Herrera's crayon note.

"Good thinking. Now we have the address, we must go right away. We can be in Tijuana by tomorrow," she said. "You're going with me, of course?"

"But we can't go just like that…." I stammered.

After studying my ten-year-old truck, Marla said, "You can drive my car. You're younger and my eyes aren't good for night driving. Don't worry, I just came back from the bank and we have tons of money to get us there and credit cards to boot. I just hope Laurita is okay. Traveling can be hard on children, you know."

"Do you think we can get down there in one day and back the next?"

She checked her watch. "If we fly," she grinned. "I have two tickets for San Jose to San Diego. I was going to bribe Mel into going with me, but now I don't have to."

At first I felt a tiny bit better about the trip until I started thinking about details. By the time we reached the airport in San Jose, I had thought of fifty reasons why we shouldn't go, like my frameless paintings, the up-coming Christmas party at my house and the fact that I had no suitcase, toothbrush or extra underwear.

But the reason for going—to find Laurita—kept me on track. I would fly to San Diego and accompany Marla to Tijuana.

We arrived at the San Jose Mineta Airport at three o'clock for our four o'clock flight. We parked, hopped a shuttle bus, stood in line, took off our shoes, got wanded and had half an hour to wait before boarding. I called David. Dear practical David agreed to take care of Solow until I got back, but failed to understand why I had to suddenly go to San Diego to fetch a little girl I barely knew. Every time I thought of Mr. Herrera sitting in his wheelchair, tears streaming down his cheeks, I knew I had to find Laurita and her mother even if it upset my dearest friend, David.

Marla and I boarded a Southwest Boeing 737. The rows of seats were nearly full, just an empty pigeon hole here and there. Marla found an aisle seat near the front. Mine was a window seat in the back. Luckily, I was a yoga expert, used to twisting into a pretzel in over-loaded seating situations. The nice lady next to me should have booked two seats instead of borrowing half of mine. Two hours and nine thousand minutes later, we landed in San Diego. I hobbled out of the plane with my foot asleep and my hip complaining.

"Isn't this wonderful?" Marla chirped as we swiftly walked the San Diego Airport corridors.

"What's so wonderful?" I gulped air.

"We don't have to pick up luggage. We can go straight to our bus."

"What bus?" Unfortunately we hadn't sat together on the plane and I had no idea what she had in mind. I only knew it was past dinner time, I was hungry and Southwest Airlines' pretzels had not helped the situation.

We exited the building onto a busy bus route. Dozens of mini- and full-size busses idled at the curb.

Marla found one with a picture of a bull fighter on the back, a pretty good hint for a Tijuana destination. She poked her head in the door and talked to the driver.

"Okay, Josephine, this is the one. It leaves in half and hour. Lets go back in and buy something to eat." We hurried back along the corridors keeping a fast pace since we had a limited amount of time. We exited the building with two bags of tacos. Marla thought they might help us get into the "Mexican mood."

As we settled into adjacent seats, the bus pulled into traffic.

"Do you think we'll find them?" I asked.

Marla checked her watch. "Yes, we'll find them. Don't worry."

"You sound so sure. How can you be so confident?" I also wondered how she kept her positive attitude through losing her sister, crashing her car and now a new disaster—Juanita and Laurita were heading for the border, running scared.

"I'm sure," she said, "because I checked my watch and it was 8:40."

"I'm lost. What does the time have to do with anything?" I scratched my head.

"It's very simple. Do you believe that your subconscious knows much more than your conscious mind?"

"Yeah, I guess so…."

"Your subconscious mind works like a computer. It knows everything, but recall isn't always the best, especially after age fifty."

"I'm experiencing some of that. I happen to be fifty." What was she leading up to?

"If a question comes to mind, I check my watch. When I add the numbers together the total must be divisible by four, or the answer is *no*. 4:40 is a yes, 4:41 is a no."

"You really believe this?" I said in a casual way, as if I'd been around people with nutty ideas all my life.

Marla smiled. "I don't use this method in life and death situations, but over the years I've had very good results. The hardest part is trusting the *yes* or *no* answer to a question."

I didn't know Marla well enough to know if she was extra smart, psychic or really stupid. But she was a nice lady so I went along with everything she said as if it was a well known fact. We finished eating our tacos, stuffed the wrappers and scraps into one bag and pushed it under the seat in front of us for lack of a garbage can.

I put my head back, closed my eyes and relaxed. A thought came to me so I shared it with Marla. "I just thought of something that might be similar to your way of answering questions with numbers."

Marla looked interested.

"Very often, when I paint murals my clients will ask me to replicate certain colors—you know, like I have to put a certain reddish color in the picture to go with the throw pillows—that sort of thing. When I go to make the various requested colors, I squirt several colors into a pot, mix it up and almost every time it matches the pillow or whatever exactly. After many years of painting, I don't consciously think about the colors and how much to use, so it must be my subconscious mind in control."

"I think you're right, Josephine, and that's why the numbers would probably work for you. Besides, I think you use your intuition a great deal."

It had been dark outside for hours, but inside the bus, people had over-head reading lights on and some worked on laptops, but most people were busy on their phones. We were a rolling electronic community of strangers crossing the border into another land, another culture. I rested my head against the back of my seat and closed my eyes. The last thing I remembered was feeling the vibration of the bus tires as they rolled south.

I dreamt I was at Disneyland in a boat on the jungle cruise ride. Someone tried to push me into the water where a giant platypus was licking his lips, waiting for me. I struggled to stay in the boat until a boa constrictor grabbed my shoulder. I opened my eyes.

"Bad dream?" Marla said, as she gave me one more wakeup shake for good measure.

"Yeah, Disneyland," I said, as my mind came back to the bus ride. I checked my watch. One half hour had gone by since we'd boarded and already we were stopped, picking up passengers.

"You were making funny noises."

"Thanks for waking me, Marla; it wasn't a good dream. Where are we?"

"Chula Vista. We should be in TJ in less than an hour."

I silently asked myself if we would be in Tijuana in less than one hour, then checked my watch. It was 7:41. My answer was *yes* according to Marla's rules because the numbers added up to twelve, a number devisable by four. I wasn't convinced of anything. I would wait to see if we really did arrive in less than an hour.

Highway 15 South became Highway 10 as we crossed the border. Ten more minutes and we were driving through Tijuana, a bustling, twinkling city full of lights, traffic and pedestrians. Even though it was 8:15 on a winter evening, the pedestrians were dressed for summer. We stopped at the bus station.

I pulled the crayon note from Pedro out of my purse.

"I'll get a cab," Marla volunteered. She finally got the attention of a young driver who helped us into his older mini-van decorated with advertisements. Three customers were already sitting inside waiting as we climbed into the far back bench seat. I buckled up and handed the crayon note to the couple in the middle seat. They sent it up to the driver who was already whipping through traffic, blowing his horn and driving at speeds fit for Nascar racing.

After many near misses, sharp turns and sudden stops, we emerged from the glitter of the city into the southern hills where good-size homes had lofty views and immaculate landscaping. It looked like Juanita came from an upper-middle-class family. Why would she put up with living conditions in a garage in America? This was not what I'd expected.

We had already dropped off the first three passengers and moved forward into their seats. The van cruised along suburban streets higher and higher into the hills. The driver finally pulled up to the curb in front of a brick house with a flat roof and an ornate iron fence around the front lawn.

Marla bartered with the driver while I opened the iron gate and walked across the lawn. Bougainvillea arched over a breeze way, front and center, that led to an inner patio and finally, an ornately carved double door. I heard children playing down the street, a dog barked far away and a couple of cars drove by the house. *Just a regular neighborhood*, I told myself.

Marla caught up to me. "Lovely night isn't it."

"Yeah, except nobody is answering the door...Oh, hi, my name is Josephine."

A tall woman in her fifties with dark hair in a stylish cut, told us in accented English that she didn't want to buy anything. Marla assured her in Spanish that we were not selling anything. She mentioned Juanita and Laurita in her next sentence. The woman's jaw went forward as her shoulders went back. Her inscrutable eyes watched us as if we were about to steal something.

Marla talked some more about Laurita and the woman's eyes softened.

"What's going on?" I asked Marla.

"Don't worry, it will be all right. She's been expecting her daughter, that's why she's up so late. I told her we're here to assure Juanita that nothing will happen to Laurita."

Juanita's mother motioned for us to sit down on the sofa while she sat on a matching over-stuffed chair emoting all the warmth of a mannequin from Macy's. Two yellow cats meandered into the room, checked us out and left. I didn't blame them. The room felt cold.

Chapter 20

Half awake, I heard voices but couldn't make out the words. A slim line of light under a door, footsteps and a weepy child signaled Juanita's arrival at her mother's home in Tijuana. Marla and I had fallen asleep in sitting positions on the sofa while the lady of the house went to bed. My foot was asleep, reminding me of the uncomfortable flight to San Diego. I wagged my foot back and forth. A cat screamed, scratched my ankle and galloped to the door. The door opened, light filtered in and a little girl peeked into our sleeping quarters.

Marla rubbed her eyes, leaped out of her seat and practically ran across the spacious room to her sweet little Laurita. She swooped up the girl and twirled her around the floor in a happy dance, Laurita's arms tight around Marla's neck. When the laughing and crying was done, they sat down next to me on the sofa. The cats joined us, but only for a minute. The felines scampered away when Juanita and her mother walked in and turned on the lights.

Juanita stood in front of Marla, hands on skinny hips, daring her to speak.

Marla spoke to Juanita calmly in Spanish, and I listened closely trying to translate her words into English. She explained to Juanita that we were the only ones who knew about Laurita being with Mary at the cliffs. The child had done nothing to cause Mary's death. The police were not after her daughter, there was no reason to run away.

For an instant Juanita's mother wore a tight smile.

Juanita came back at Marla spitting out an angry English and Spanish mixture of words. She accused Mary of giving dangerous pain killers to her husband who could not stop taking them. She accused Mary of ruining her life the night of the crash. It was Mary's fault that her husband could not work, let alone walk. She was angry that she had to work the night shift in a smelly convalescent hospital for very little pay.

Marla cut her off by naming all the things Mary had done for the family such as a free place to live, free child care, even a used bicycle to ride to work and to the store.

Suddenly, I remembered seeing the back of the bike Juanita rode to work. A dark blue knapsack or backpack was strapped to the back fender. My face flushed and my heart pounded.

The women continued arguing.

Juanita's mother kept still. I wondered where she stood. Did she love her daughter? Did she know bad things about her from the past? I imagined Juanita had been a difficult child.

"Juanita, were you at the cliffs the day Mary died?" I asked.

Her eyes flared as she gave me a fiendish smile. In perfect English she said, "Of course I was there. I hated that woman. She ruined my life." Quick as a bolt of lightening, Juanita grabbed Laurita's hand and dragged her through the house to the back door, stopping only to grab her mother's purse from the kitchen. Her mother was too stunned to move, but Marla and I were only steps behind Juanita as she ran into the garage, tossed the little girl into the front seat of a black car, climbed in and locked the doors.

Laurita looked up at us from the passenger seat, tears runny down her cheeks. No child's seat or even a seatbelt for her safety.

The instant the garage door opened, the black Mercedes shot down the short driveway, made a right, and the tail lights disappeared into the night.

We went back to the mother to ask for her help, but she just stared at the Oriental rug under her bare feet. Marla gently took the woman's arm and led her to the sofa where she sat down to recover her dignity.

After a long silence, she said, "Senoras, I have forgotten my manners, come," and she led us into the kitchen where she opened the refrigerator, pointing here and there. In Spanish she rambled on and then in English asked if we were hungry.

Marla translated, saying, "Her cook won't be here until eight in the morning and she wants to know if you would like a beef or pork sandwich."

I checked my watch. It was almost two o'clock in the morning and my stomach couldn't remember having tacos at the airport.

"Pork would be nice," I said, wondering where the tacos and burritos were hidden. We ate our sandwiches and discussed how we might get Laurita away from the crazed Juanita. The mother listened, poured herself a tall beer and chugged it down like a sailor. Did she understand that her daughter had murdered a woman named Mary?

Marla was more adamant than ever about getting Laurita back to her father, begging the woman for information about where Juanita might be going.

The woman didn't object, she just gulped two shots of tequila which ultimately loosened her tongue and her tears.

"Don't worry, Josephine," said Marla, "she said she thinks Juanita will probably go to her younger sister's apartment in San Diego where she attends San Diego State. She gave me the address and everything. I'll call a cab." By the time the cab arrived, the woman of the house was into the second half of a bottle of sherry.

A horn tooted at the curb.

Our goodbyes and thank yous went unanswered as Marla and I rushed out the front door and hopped into a yellow minivan driven by a gentleman wearing a blue uniform and a handlebar mustache. He spoke English with a heavy accent.

I buckled up, pulled Sheriff Sayer's card from my wallet and punched his number into my cell phone. He answered on the second ring—at two-thirty in the morning!

"Officer Sayer, this is Josephine Stuart…."

"Okay, I'm listening."

"I have proof positive that Juanita Herrera murdered Mary Christmas…I mean, Mary Milford. She's in San Diego with her daughter…driving around without even a seat belt to protect her little girl. We think she's holed up at her sister's apartment at 505 Hardy Avenue. It's near San Diego State…."

"Thank you, Ms. Stuart, now get some sleep." He hung up.

"Get some sleep?!" I snapped.

Marla rolled her eyes. "He didn't take you seriously, did he?"

The cabbie looked at me in the rearview mirror.

After a short ride to our destination in San Diego, Marla paid the driver. We climbed out of the cab, walked a few yards up a well-lit sidewalk and entered the foyer of a modern three-story apartment house. The well-lit entry had a tile floor, high ceiling and no furniture. A long wall on our left was nothing but metal mailboxes with keyholes. Mounted on the opposite wall was a glass case containing a registry of all the renters and their phone numbers, which was useless to us because no one had ever mentioned Juanita's sister's name.

A few frustrating minutes ticked by.

We heard someone coming and turned to look at the door where we'd entered. A tall leather-from-head-to-toe young man walked past us, stopped to check his mail and started to leave through a door at the other end of the room.

"Excuse me," I said.

He looked at us for the first time.

"We need to find apartment Number 332. How do we find it?"

Leather legs looked down, smiled and motioned for us to follow him through the security door. We entered a room just long enough to house three elevators. Legs walked up to the last one, pressed a green button, the door opened and he motioned for us to join him inside. He probably thought we were a couple of nuts wandering around at three-thirty in the morning. After a very quick ride, the door opened on the third floor. Our friend-of-few-words used his key on door Number 331. Before he went inside, he thumbed the door across the hall, Number 332.

We paused in front of the door and listened. I heard nothing but the hum of the ice machine down the hall.

"Do we have a plan, Josephine?" Marla whispered.

"No, but my adrenaline is sure pumping. Now that we're here, I'm thinking we might be crazy to go up against Juanita and her sister. They're obviously a lot younger and one of them is a killer. Think about it, she has nothing to lose."

"I've thought of nothing else, Josephine, but I must take Laurita home to her father. He's not a bad father, he's just depressed. And I'd never forgive myself if something happened to his little girl."

"Okay, here goes." I knocked on the door, lightly at first.

Finally the door opened a crack. Dark eyes peeked out.

Marla didn't wait to be invited in. Using the element of surprise, she stepped back and lurched forward, throwing her body at the door, pushing it open enough for us to enter.

A college-age girl wearing only a long t-shirt and mussed up long black hair tried to scream but only a squeak came out.

"Don't worry," I said. "This is Marla and I'm Josephine and we're here to help you."

"Huh?" she croaked. "This is my apartment; what are you doing here?"

Something moved in the dimly lit room that obviously served as kitchen, dining room and living room. Someone behind the sofa whimpered. We knew at once Laurita was hiding there. But where was her mother? Straight across the room was an open sliding glass door and a small balcony overlooking the pool.

Marla grabbed my shirt. "Where are you going?"

"I'll check out the balcony, you see if she's in the bedroom." I cautiously stepped onto the balcony and looked around. The centrally-located swimming pool was blocked in by apartments on all four sides and flooded with light. By contrast, the balcony was dark as a coal mine. All of a sudden someone grabbed my hair and twisted my head in a direction it couldn't go. I tried to scream, but I was roughly thrown to the concrete floor. I pulled myself up using the metal railing, but someone had my ankles. As I clung to the top rail, my legs were flung over the top. I gripped the cold metal with one hand and then two as my legs dangled twenty feet above yards of concrete. Deck chairs, tables and umbrellas littered the area directly below.

So this was December in San Diego. Strange thoughts ran through my mind. I felt dizzy. Every important person and event in my life flashed through my heightened consciousness. Where was Marla? Why wasn't anyone helping me?

"Help!" I shouted, but it was a weak shout because someone was bashing my fingers with a shoe. My hands slipped slowly down the rails to where the metal entered the balcony's concrete floor.

I shouted for help again.

A light flickered on in an apartment just below my feet. Random windows turned yellow surrounding the pool. I heard people talking on their balconies and saw flashes from their camera phones.

Wack! Wack! The shoe kept hitting my fingers. At some point it would be unbearable and I'd have to let go. I would probably break my neck when I landed on the concrete, or at least my legs. I asked God to help me. The first thing that came to mind was, "God helps those who help themselves." I began swinging my body back and forth, harder and harder. The shoe never stopped. When I could hold on not another minute, I took an even longer swing and let go of the rail, aiming my body in the direction of the pool, saying goodbye to Mom, Dad, and David.

As I fell through the air, the last sound I heard was a distant siren. If only I could have held on a little longer….

Chapter 21

If I was dead, I definitely didn't make it to heaven. I couldn't open my eyes, I couldn't feel my feet, my shoulder had a dull ache in it and the air smelled like Lysol, rubbing alcohol and dog poop. I had smelled that odor before…in a hospital. I knew I wasn't alone, unless the voices I heard were in my head, which would mean I'd landed far south of heaven.

Someone touched my arm. Ouch, that was a shot! But I was too tired to object or even cry. I tried to open my mouth, but something was already in it, some tubes or something. Someone talked to me saying, "AAggoolaammee." I gave up trying to listen and fell back into my personal abyss.

The next time I was conscious it was because someone was speaking to me. This time I heard actual words. "Are you comfortable? Don't move, I'm going to remove some bandages and uncover your eyes. Don't move."

I wished I could move, but I was all tied down like a mummy under sheets cemented to the floor. As they unwrapped my head, more and more light seeped through my eyelids. But that light was nothing compared to opening my eyes for the first time since, since, ah…*oh well*, I thought, I couldn't think about the recent past because I simply had no memory of it. Thankfully, I was able to remember Mom and Dad, my first husband Marty, the kitten I'd found when I was in Miss Larson's fourth grade class, adopting Solow as a puppy and my first kiss from David.

"Ms. Stuart, you can open your eyes now," a woman's voice said.

Instead, I opened my mouth and found that I was able to speak. My words came from a dry, scratchy throat. "Will it hurt to open my eyes?" I asked, not knowing why they were closed in the first place.

"Maybe a little bit, but you should try to open your eyes," a male voice said.

I held my breath and opened one eye, then the other. "What's the big deal?" I said, looking up at a woman doctor and her side-kick male nurse. It looked like they were holding their breath. Mr. balding in scrubs handed me a hand-mirror. *Why would I want that?* I asked myself.

"Oh my God!" My jaw dropped. "Ouch!" I gulped some air, trying to remember what I used to look like before I had raccoon eyes and black stitches across my chin.

"Ms. Stuart…."

"Josephine," I said.

"Josephine, you're going to be just fine. You injured your spleen and while we were operating on that, we found a small ganglion growth and removed it." The doctor smiled. "It saved you from big problems later."

"Other than my face and spleen, what happened to me?"

"Miraculously, you escaped with just twelve stitches on the back of your head, concussion, a twisted ankle, two fractured toes, bruises and a few contusions—nothing life threatening," she said, as she double-checked my chart posted at the end of the bed. "Are you aware of any memory problems?"

"Yes, I'm having lots of memory problems. I don't know how I got so messed up. Was I in a car accident?"

The nurse rolled his eyes, smiled and left the room.

The doctor read from my chart. "Patient experienced severe trauma to head and trunk after falling from a third floor balcony. Patient landed partially on lounge chair which rolled into a swimming pool. Patient was resuscitated and transported by ENTs."

"Sounds like I was the life of the party," I quipped.

The doctor frowned.

"I'm just kidding. I don't remember how I happened to fall three stories, but I'm sure it was not a party." Every time I tried to recall what happened, all I remembered was being very afraid, staring into blackness and hearing my own heartbeat. I had a flicker of a memory of being on an airplane.

"Ms. Stuart, do you feel up to seeing a very persistent visitor?"

"I guess so. Who is it?"

David must have been listening to us from the hall. He poked his head in the door and said, "Hi, Josie."

The doctor left us alone. David very carefully kissed my forehead and started to fill me in on what had happened.

"So you say I'm in San Diego? Why would I be in San Diego?"

"Honey, you flew down here with your friend, Marla to try to find Laurita and bring her back to her father."

"Okay…if you say so. Did we find Laurita?"

"Marla has already taken the little girl back to Capitola. She stayed here with you until I arrived, and Bob and Leola are in the waiting room. You gave us a pretty big scare." I knew he meant it by the concern in his shaky voice.

"Why would Laurita go to San Diego and who did she go with? Oh, it must have been her mother, right?" The image of an old bike with an ooga horn popped into my head.

"Are you starting to remember?" his voice cracked.

"Actually, I'm too tired to try to remember," I yawned.

David adjusted my pillow, bent down and kissed me on my forehead and left the room. I don't know how much time passed, but when I woke up, I saw two people bent over my beat-up body, checking me out.

"Oh dear, we didn't mean to wake you," Mom said.

"Yes, we did," Dad corrected her. "We came all this way to see you and we want to know how you're feeling." His jaw was set and a big worry line ran across his brow.

"I'm okay. I can't feel a thing—just feeling a little loopy. Did they tell you that I had surgery?"

"We know," Mom said, trying to keep her voice under control. "We talked to Alicia on the phone. Is there anyone else you'd like us to call?"

"Not really," I sighed. "I just want to go home."

Dad reached for my hand, the one without all the tubing.

"Ouch! What's wrong with my hands? Why are they taped up?"

"Honey," he said, "your hands need to heal along with the rest of your body. The doctor told us you'll need another three or four days. They want to get you home before Christmas and we're counting on it. I have plane tickets for the three of us on Christmas Eve. You can't imagine the hoops I had to go through to get them—seems everyone wants to travel on that day."

Mom rolled her eyes.

"I have no concept of time right now. How long have I been here?"

Mom leaned down and held a cup of cool water to my lips. I sipped.

"Honey, they brought you in Thursday and today is Saturday."

"Wasn't I supposed to do something Saturday?"

The room went dead quiet. A nagging feeling rattled my brain. Whatever it was would have to wait. My eyelids felt heavy. The abyss welcomed me.

The next time I woke up, the window to my right was black except for distant city lights. I remembered the old days when I was a child. Giant spotlights pointed toward the stars advertising new buildings, a new car lot or a wonderful new movie at the Paramount Theater. Going to the city was exciting, especially around Christmas time when all the big department stores decorated their huge front windows with moving elves, flying angels and laughing Santas.

It finally occurred to me that Christmas was coming soon. I remembered Marla calling her sister, "Mary Christmas," the family's nickname because of Mary's fascination with the holiday season as demonstrated by her elaborate collection of decorations. I remembered seeing the stack of boxes labeled, "Christmas Decorations" in Mary's bedroom and more in the closet.

Lying in bed with nothing to do, I tried to remember the past week. All I was able to remember was Marla rolling her SUV in a lettuce field. I couldn't remember specifics, but I had a feeling Marla and I were finally good friends. I understood how much she missed her sister and it was very clear how much she loved little Laurita.

Someone entered my room.

I opened my eyes. It was my favorite nurse, Lucy, the one who seemed to love her job. She smiled a lot and hummed a little tune as she checked my vitals, etc. She cheerfully talked about movies, music, her favorite restaurants and her boyfriend. She handed me an article she'd cut out of the *San Diego Union-Tribune*. I glanced at the picture of a woman dangling from a balcony.

"Was this on Utube?" I asked.

Lucy nodded.

"TV news?"

She laughed. "At least you weren't wearing a dress."

"That was the only thing going my way," I said, feeling pain in my fingers. Was I starting to remember something?

"Ms. Josephine, do you need anything before I shut off the lights?"

"Yes, I'd like to wear my watch...."

"But Miss, the clock is right there on the wall," the chubby blond nurse said.

"I would really like to wear my watch."

"It's against the rules…but I'll see what I can do," she winked. She dug through a large plastic bag full of my clothing and purse, and found a small bag containing a ring and a watch. She presented the watch to me, probably wondering what was so special about an ordinary Timex.

I checked the time. 9:30 exactly. According to Marla's method, it amounted to a healthy yes—yes, I should wear my watch.

"Miss, if you're not too sleepy, I can give you a letter."

"I'm not sleepy at all. I slept most of the day."

With her usual smile, she pulled a stamped envelope from her smock pocket and handed it to me. The return address was 1430 Jade Street, Capitola. I was so happy and excited to get a letter from Marla, I didn't even notice another nurse coming at me with a loaded syringe.

"This will help you to sleep," she chirped.

"But I really want to read this letter."

"I'll help you with that," Lucy said. She grabbed the envelope and ripped it open easily after I had struggled long and hard with no results. I was pathetic, no strength for anything.

Hoping to finish reading the letter before the shot put me down, I ignored the nurse's efforts to straighten my sheets and blanket.

Dear Josephine,

I hope you are recovering nicely. I left for home Friday after being in phone contact with Pedro. Laurita and I flew into San Jose Airport Friday afternoon. You can't imagine how happy and sad Pedro was, getting his daughter back and losing his wife. She is being held by the San Diego Police. At first, Juanita's sister held me back from helping you, but later understood what we were up against and was very nice to me. She was as afraid of her sister as we were.

Do you remember the young man wearing leather who helped us find Room 332? Well, he heard what was happening across the hall and ran down to the pool just in time to pull you out of the water. That's when the fire department arrived and resuscitated you. I was afraid you wouldn't make it. The police caught Juanita as she ran out of the building and took her into custody.

Thank you for helping me find Laurita. She says "hi."

Hope to see you soon.

Sincerely,

Marla

Four hours later, I woke up for my blood pressure testing and another shot. I was a human pincushion. *Was all this necessary?* I asked myself. I checked my watch. It was 2:20 a.m., a positive answer to my question. Feeling like I had a handle on this numbers thing, I asked myself if the syringe-wielding night nurse hated me and checked the time, 2:22. No, she didn't hate me. She was just doing her job.

Every time I needed to go to the bathroom I pushed a button and a nurse would arrive, usually Lucy, and she would help me across the room. It was only a few steps, but I wasn't steady on my feet. Sunday afternoon Lucy presented me with a walker so that I could make the trip on my own.

After only four days in the hospital, I had become institutionalized. I didn't notice the chemical smells and bad tasting food any more and I could sleep amongst lights and noisy people. Like a rat in a cage, I did what I was told to do.

My bedside phone rang Sunday afternoon, interrupting one of my many naps. I answered it.

"Allie, hi! I'm so glad you called. You have to break me out of this place."

"Wish I could, Jo, but I'm home with my family. I called to tell you about the Art Festival."

"Oh my gosh, that was Saturday night. I knew something important was happening. How did you do?"

"Fine. I sold three paintings. Not bad for a first try, don't you think?"

"Yeah, that's terrific," I said with as much enthusiasm as I could conjure up.

"And five of your paintings sold."

"What are you talking about, Allie?"

"Buzz called me. He was looking for you because he had eight frames with mats all ready for you to pick up. I arranged to pick them up and since you never lock your doors, I found your paintings and framed them for you. We had a nice looking show Saturday."

I could hardly speak. What a wonderful friend Alicia was. She knew how important the art show was to me. I tried to thank her.

"You would have done the same for me. Now get yourself well!"

David flew home Sunday night. He kissed me goodbye before he left and acted like he didn't want to leave, but he said his son, Harley and granddaughter, Monica, were going to spend Christmas with him and he needed to straighten up the house before they arrived. He had a plane ticket and off he went.

I still had Mom and Dad popping in at odd times between their activities at the hotel, asking if I needed anything. They had rented a room by the ocean, joined a senior aerobics class, did some deep sea fishing and attended a roller derby competition.

I cringed at the thought of two more days of hospital food, two more days until I would be set free. What if my memory never came back? What if my stitches broke? Would I survive this ordeal? I checked my watch. It was 10:30, time to go to sleep, and sure enough, here came the loaded syringe.

Chapter 22

My first visitors Monday morning had sailing on their minds. Mom and Dad had teamed up with a younger couple from their aerobics class at the hotel for a day of sailing. They tried not to look bored and ready to run out the hospital door, but I'd known them for fifty years and they were so bored. I sent them on their way, reassuring them over and over that I was fine and just wanted to rest.

When my folks were gone and the nurses had sponged me down, recorded my vitals and finally left me alone, I took a look at the newspaper article Lucy had given me. Once I got past the photograph of a fifty-year-old woman dangling from a balcony, I read the article twice, not believing what I had read. I was outraged. How could they get it so wrong?

According to the article, "Juanita Herrera was set free on her own recognizance after being arrested for attacking Josephine Stuart, a resident of Aromas, California." It went on to describe how I lost the fight by falling off the balcony into a swimming pool. There was no mention of murder charges in Santa Cruz County.

I pressed my emergency button several times.

Lucy ran into the room expecting something awful.

"Lucy, please bring me my purse. This is an emergency."

Poor Lucy looked dumb-struck. "What emergency?" she asked, looking this way and that for a loose snake or fire in the curtains.

"The article you gave me—they have it all wrong. A killer is out on her own recognizance and I have to warn my friend, Marla. I just hope it's not too late."

Lucy set my purse down beside me on the bed. My bandaged right hand dug through the faux gator purse until it found my mini-address book. I asked Lucy to dial the phone as I called out the numbers.

She dialed and handed me the phone.

"Hi, Marla; it's me, Josephine…."

"How are you feeling, dear?"

"Never mind that; Juanita is free—they set her free! You need to keep Laurita with you and keep Mel around and Buzz and Ricky. She's strong and crazy and I think she's going to try to get Laurita back…."

"Thanks for the warning, Josephine. I'll be very careful." I felt better when I heard fear and then resolve in Marla's voice.

My next call was to Officer Sayer.

"Ms. Stuart, might you be calling about the article in the *Sentinel* today?"

"You mean about me falling from the balcony…?"

He chuckled. I presume the woman who attacked you is the one you're accusing in the murder of Mary Milford."

"You got that right, and the newspapers got it all wrong. They make it look like I was in a drunken girl-fight. Juanita tried to kill me by throwing me off the balcony. It's a wonder I didn't die. But the worst part of this situation is that the police didn't take her seriously and now she's out of jail. You need to get some protection going for Marla Milford at 1430 Jade Street. Juanita Herrera is going to go looking for her daughter."

"Are you saying that your friend Marla has Ms. Herrera's daughter?"

"The father has the daughter, but Marla lives in the same house…."

"And Marla is what relation to the father?"

"A friend, that's all," I said and hung up.

Next, I called Alicia, told her the situation and asked if she and Ernie could check on Marla now and then. She said they would. Alicia was already feeding Solow and Fluffy until David got home.

Finally, I could relax. I gazed at the blue sky and green hills outside my window. Two more days and I would be out there in the big beautiful world….

"Hey, what's that for? I already had a…ouch, that hurt!" I grumped at the nurse with a scarf over her head and evil eyes I recognized. She darted out the door as I began pushing the panic button and yelling at the top of my voice.

Poor Lucy hurried into the room.

"Lucy, Juanita just gave me a shot in my arm. She's not a nurse and she's getting away…and I feel awful…." Within minutes, everything went black except a small light and then the light went out. I couldn't speak. The abyss welcomed me.

Consciousness happened slowly. I heard noises, but was too tired to open my eyes. Did I make it to heaven this time? No, because I smelled Lysol, rubbing alcohol and dog poop. I had a fuzzy memory of Juanita grabbing my arm. Did she shoot me up with something bad? I finally opened my eyes and checked my watch. The numbers were too blurry to read. I wondered what that meant in Marla's world.

"Josephine, it's Lucy, can you hear me?"

I tried to speak but my lips were too tired.

The next time I woke up, it was 2:00 in the afternoon. I noticed a new tube attached to my arm. At least time was passing, I was alive and Lucy arrived carrying a tall glass of orange juice for me to drink.

"I was so worried about you," Lucy said. "It seems the woman impersonating a nurse gave you a dose of insulin. One of the nurses found the syringe in a garbage can on the first floor. Your doctor figured out what had happened and quickly went to work, even before the syringe had been tested. She saved you with an injection of glucagon and then another one later on. We weren't sure...oh dear. I didn't think you would make it." She sniffed.

"Did Juanita get away?"

"No, an announcement was made on the intercom and the security guys caught her on the first floor as she tried to leave the building. Maybe this time the police will keep her. They wanted to know when they could question you." Lucy adjusted my pillow. "Don't worry, I'll keep them away...."

"No, no, I want to tell them everything." I sipped orange juice from a straw. "And the sooner the better." An old adage crossed my mind, be careful what you wish for, as I watched two police officers enter my little room.

Lucy slipped out the door.

"Ms. Stuart?" the tallest officer asked.

"Yes, is it true you caught Juanita Herrera?" I asked.

"We'll ask the questions, ma'am," the second officer said with tons of authority in his young voice. "Will you be pressing charges?"

"Yes, I will." I held up my ravaged knuckles, recently unwrapped, as specimen 'A.' "This was her first attempt at killing me." I knew my raccoon eyes had cleared up, but my hands would need more time to heal completely. I pulled up the sleeve of my gown exposing my shoulder, showing them some really ugly purple and yellow bruises.

The youngest officer emitted an involuntary grunt, obviously creeped out by my colorful skin.

The other officer looked at the clock and back to me. "We have your phone number and address in A..Roe..Mass, California. We'll be in touch."

"Wait, don't you want to know about Mary?"

Two blank looks stared back at me.

"Juanita Herrera murdered Mary Milford about a month ago by pushing her off a cliff into the ocean…."

"Ma'am, the Santa Cruz Police Department will handle that charge."

"But Mary's murder has everything to do with my case. Juanita knows that I know who killed Mary."

"Don't worry, ma'am," the younger officer said. "She won't get out of jail this time."

I wasn't convinced, but what else could I do?

The officers left and Lucy came back in the room.

"Did she really kill someone?" Lucy had obviously listened to us from the hallway.

"Yes, and Mary was a very nice person. Her family called her Mary Christmas because she loved the holidays, especially Christmas, and she decorated extensively every year. That reminds me, I need to call Marla."

Lucy handed me the phone. I had memorized Marla's number. She picked up right away, sounding breathless.

"Hi, Marla; it's Josephine. You can stop worrying; Juanita is back in jail."

"That's wonderful, but why is she in if they just let her out? I'm confused."

"She tried to kill me by shooting me up with insulin." I heard Marla gasp. "Juanita would make a terrible nurse. That shot really hurt…but not for long. My doctor did some quick work on me, saved my life actually and the hospital security guards captured Juanita and the police took her to the pokey."

"Oh dear, you've been through so much, Josephine. If it helps, Laurita is fine—hardly misses her mother. I didn't want to say anything at first, but now I will. Juanita was not a good mother. I talked to Pedro and he wants me to help him raise Laurita. I'm thrilled, as you can imagine. Now I know what my retirement will look like. You get some rest, dear, and we'll talk soon."

Suddenly I was exhausted. My head hit the pillow and in no time I was out. I dreamt there were dozens of elves wearing green nurse's scrubs and big white shoes, sliding down giant candy canes into a swimming pool full of sharks. I tried to warn the little nurses but all that came out of my mouth was a whisper. Everyone ignored me. Finally I decided I must be wrong about the sharks. I should give the elves the benefit of the doubt and have a swim with them. But one shark looked familiar. Its eyes were Juanita's eyes. I looked around for help and realized all the sharks looked like Mary's killer.

Chapter 23

Tuesday morning, I woke up feeling like I'd turned a corner healthwise. My shoulder didn't hurt and the backs of my hands didn't look like raw meat any more. Lucy fluttered around the room. She rewrapped my broken toes, pulled out the tube in my arm and asked questions about my confrontation with Juanita, which I was finally able to remember. I felt deeply grateful to be alive as I recalled everything that had happened in Tijuana and San Diego.

"Looks like you'll be leaving this place, since you're able to walk the halls and make your own bed," Lucy laughed. "And I see you ate everything and stacked your breakfast dishes."

"Nervous energy, I guess. You've been great, Lucy. What are your plans for Christmas?"

"I'll be right here at the hospital—skeleton staff and all that. I don't mind because I'm not married with children. I'll enjoy a late supper with my folks after work." Lucy fussed around a bit longer, but left the room when Mom and Dad arrived. They seemed happy to see me walking around without tubing and a rolling cart shadowing me.

"We take off for home at four o'clock," Dad said. "What would you like to do around San Diego?"

Mom jabbed him with her elbow. "Bob, don't be ridiculous; she's in no condition…."

"I just thought lunch at the waterfront might be nice. We don't have to turn in the rental car until two o'clock. It's a beautiful seventy degrees outside, might as well enjoy San Diego while we can." He winked at me.

Suddenly I had a yearning for a big shrimp salad. By the time my doctor checked me out of the hospital, we barely had time to drive to the waterfront and eat a quick lunch before taking the car back to the airport that was jam packed with travelers making last minute trips to be with family and friends for Christmas. Mom and Dad insisted I ride in a wheelchair through the airport and eased me through the crowds, acting as buffers and helpers every step of the way.

Our plane was a half hour late arriving at the San Diego Airport, not bad compared to many other planes that day.

I called David to let him know that I would be home soon.

Once we boarded the plane, it was another forty minutes sitting on the tarmac before we were cleared to take off. Like a time machine going from summer to winter, we flew away from warm sunny San Diego into cold windy San Jose. As we disembarked, we pulled on our jackets and claimed Mom and Dad's one little suitcase from the luggage carousel. From there, we caught a mini-bus that took us to Mom's Subaru parked in long-term parking.

Dad took the wheel. The pace was stop, go and slower than slow. Normally it would be a one hour drive home, but Christmas Eve has never been "normal times."

It was eight-thirty when we finally drove up the driveway to my house. The lights were on and smoke billowed from the chimney. David heard us and opened the front door. The first hug lasted long, the second one even longer. I had forgotten how good he smelled, like soap, shaving cream and bubble gum.

Solow tried to get between us, whipping his tail against our legs and howling a serious, "hello."

"Anything we can do for you, Honey, before we go home?" Mom asked.

"I'll be fine, thanks. I'm sorry there won't be a party tomorrow…."

"Oh yes, there will be a party—at my house," David said.

"Really, you're having us over?"

"Yes, he is," Dad said, looking like the proverbial cat that ate the canary.

We hugged and the folks took off for Santa Cruz.

My mind worked hard bringing me up to speed on past events, but I couldn't help feeling disconnected from my old life in Aromas. Can a person change in just one week? So much had happened in a short amount of time. It's not everyday one almost dies at the hands of a lunatic woman gone mad—twice. My concussion not only had scrambled my memory, it had dislocated my sense of normalcy. But David's caring ways and Solow's neediness slowly brought me back to my former good life in Aromas.

After much yawning on my part, David walked me down the hall to my bedroom. My eyes were already heavy. We kissed, he tucked me in and I curled up on my comfy new mattress, instantly asleep and dreaming about Santa bringing me a giant sack full of red roses.

Wednesday morning arrived with sunshine streaming through my bedroom windows. I had slept soundly for ten hours, making up for the interrupted tries at sleep in a hospital full of noise, lights, injections and sucky plastic tubing. My bedroom smelled of cedar, pine and roses. Oh my gosh! Roses! I hadn't noticed the dozen red roses in a milk glass vase that David must have left on my nightstand. I sniffed the roses one more time, stretched, yawned and finally bounced out of bed feeling like a woman half my age.

Solow waddled into the room and woofed that he needed to go outside. I let him out and watched his short chubby legs churn up the dirt at full speed, close behind Fluffy.

I drank coffee and read the paper, feeling relaxed and ready to visit David and his family later in the day. Christmas would happen without my cooking and planning. I wondered what kind of Christmas David would put together. Actually, he was a better cook than I ever was and his son, Harley, was even better than his dad.

Suddenly my mind went back to the front page of the newspaper I had been reading. How had I missed the bold headlines announcing Juanita Herrera's capture? The reporter wrote that she admitted she murdered Mary Milford and later attacked Josephine Stuart.

I called Marla to ask if she'd seen the article and to wish her a happy holiday but she didn't answer the phone so I left a message, same with Mel. My next call was to Alicia. She answered and wished me a happy Christmas but didn't have time to talk. She said she had some last minute shopping to do. I wondered what stores stayed open on Christmas day. Before she hung up, I asked her what had happened to the painting of Fluffy that I'd planned to frame and give to David. She said she felt awful, but that she'd framed and sold the painting at the Art Festival.

Now it was unanimous; I had nothing to give to my family and friends or to David and his family for Christmas. I hoped everyone would understand why I didn't have time to shop. I promised myself I would be more responsible next year.

My next-to-last call was to David to find out what time the party started. He said to come over any time after four, but he was too busy to talk so I called Mom and Dad. I told them to come over at four o'clock, but they seemed to know that already and were very busy making stuffed mushrooms for the party.

Feeling rather useless, I buckled a leash to Solow's collar and took him for a walk up Otis Road a few blocks. Too late, I decided to take it easy and save my energy for Christmas dinner at David's. Solow and I were both panting, my cheeks were red and my two broken toes ached as we entered the house. I flopped onto the couch and turned on the TV. Solow settled down for a nap close by. The twelve o'clock news came on.

"Oh my God!" I said to Solow, who didn't even look up. "That's Juanita wearing handcuffs!" I sat up straight to watch the "perp-walk" and the rest of the news report. Juanita didn't look pretty in her baggy orange jump-suit. The gentleman reporting said Ms. Herrera had admitted to pushing Mary Milford off a cliff in Capitola. He said she was captured by the police in San Diego and would be extradited to Santa Cruz in the next two weeks.

I wasn't hungry but it was lunch time so I slapped bologna and cheese on a toasted bagel and poured a cup of tea. Solow had discriminating taste and stayed in the living room. Halfway through my lunch, Solow barked and ran to the door. I opened it expecting to see David, not a little white-bearded man wearing a red and gold forty-niner shirt and sweat pants.

Emmett Hooley, my elderly neighbor from the other end of Otis Road, had walked to my house to give me a gift. I invited him in and we sat in the living room discussing old times. I hadn't seen him in months, but here he was, giving me a beautifully wrapped gift. As the shiny paper fell away, I discovered an adorable wood carving of Solow. It fit in the palm of my hand and went straight to my heart.

"Emmett, this is so sweet of you…." I sputtered.

"I hope the Christmas for you is good," he said in his German accent. We hugged and he left. But the warmth stayed, lasting for hours while I rested and later dressed to go to David's house for dinner. I didn't even know what my boyfriend was serving, but I knew he could find his way around a kitchen. He didn't need me.

As I touched up my hairdo with a squirt of hairspray, I heard the doorbell ring and headed to the front door wondering why Solow wasn't barking. I opened the door and Solow wagged his tail.

Chapter 24

It was exactly four o'clock Christmas day when I opened the front door to see who was there.

"Marla? I mean come in, sit down. Wow, you're all dressed up…."

"Hi, Josephine." She gave me a warm hug. Laurita peeked at me from behind Marla's long magenta and silver print skirt.

"Laurita, hi," I said.

She smiled and ducked back behind the folds of Marla's colorful skirt.

"I came by to see if you wanted to ride over to David's house with us."

"How thoughtful. I would love to ride with you. Just a minute, let me get my purse and a jacket." It was sweet of David to invite Marla and Laurita to his party so that Monica would have another five-year-old to play with. Marla and I would have a lot to talk about—the party wouldn't be dull.

Marla helped Laurita into her car seat and buckled her in.

I hefted Solow onto the floor in front of Laurita. She giggled.

It seemed like a lot of fuss for a very short trip. I opened the door to the passenger seat and was surprised to see the seat already filled. The bigger surprise was that Pedro sat in the seat holding a homemade pie in his lap.

"Ola, Josephina…marry Chreesmas," he smiled.

"Merry Christmas, Pedro. Nice to see you out and about." I rounded the car and opened the other backseat door only to find the seat already filled.

"Hi, Josephine, it's only a block—sit on my lap." Mel extended his hand. I took it and climbed up onto his lap. Two minutes and one hot flash later, we parked in front of David's house beside Mom's Subaru. Mel pulled a wheelchair from the back of the SUV, loaded Pedro into it and pushed him up to a porch decorated in colorful lights and hanging snowflakes.

A white Mustang wearing blue racing stripes pulled in behind Marla's car. Buzz, Claudia and Vick clamored out of the car. As the group walked up to David's front door, the Quintana's Volvo station wagon pulled in beside Buzz' Mustang. Alicia caught up to me on the porch and wished me a merry Christmas. Ernie was right behind her carrying a huge tray of something that smelled like homemade tamales covered with sheets of aluminum foil.

Tansey shot out of the car straight to her friend, Solow. Trigger herded them both over to the porch where David greeted everyone as they entered the house. How handsome he looked, his thick salt and pepper hair against his red sweater and charcoal cords.

My little long-sleeved black dress and red scarf had been thrown together at the last minute to hide the remaining bruises.

"Allie, where did all these people come from? Do they all know David?"

"They all know you," she smiled. "He wanted you to have a nice Christmas after all you've been through. Marla donated Mary's Christmas decorations and Coco and Moses volunteered to perform their music. I apologize for going through your address book in the kitchen drawer…."

We hugged. "Allie, you're the greatest friend a person could have. I know you had a big hand in this...thank you so much."

After a warm embrace from David, I walked through a highly decorated living room and out the sliding glass doors onto the patio. Christmas lights circled and crisscrossed high above a large expanse of slate patio, bordered by long benches and a nicely trimmed hedge. Two tall rental heaters worked to keep people warm, although at four-thirty in the afternoon the air was quite comfortable. The temperature dipped half an hour later when the sun went down.

Someone screamed.

We all looked to our left, toward the waterfall and hot tub. Someone screamed again and everyone crowded around the tub and looked down. A knitted cap floated on top of the steamy water. Was someone under the hat? While everyone discussed whether a person might be drowning, Robert jumped in. He held up his nephew's hat, but that was all he found. I felt sorry for the twins once Robert got hold of them. In the meantime he would use the beach towel David handed him and stand under one of the heaters until he was dry.

Someone laughed.

Everyone looked around to see who was snickering. Robert's nephew was hatless and his niece held a hand over her mouth trying not to laugh. Robert didn't look happy.

"That's not a nice joke to pull," Myrtle said and huffed herself back to the kitchen where Mom and Dad were serving up hot cider and adult beverages. I thought I ought to help out, but they told me to circulate and have fun.

I turned to go and bumped square into a tall, dark, shaved headed and uniformed Marine named Justin. My eyes watered when I realized who it was. He grinned and hugged me. Justin pulled his lady-friend over to meet me. She said they had only been married five weeks and five days. He would be deployed soon. Her voice sounded sweet and confident that he would be all right and return home to her. I felt so happy for the young couple.

"Justin, are you still living at Drew Lake?"

"Yes we are. I always loved it there—mostly because it reminds me of my granddaddy. By the way, we heard all about your adventures in San Diego. Are you doin' okay?" he asked, as he put an arm around his wife.

"A little sore here and there," I said, "but feeling lucky to be alive."

From across the dining room, I heard a voice that made my whole body smile. It was my Aunt Clara, Mom's younger sister, whom I had not seen since her wedding six months ago. Her husband, Ben, saw me coming and lifted me up in the air like I was a piece of balsa wood. Aunt Clara squealed and we hugged and hugged. In that joyous moment I vowed to visit them more often.

"My dear, you're looking younger every time I see you," Clara said.

"Josephine," Ben chimed in, "you need to come up to Boulder Creek and see the old place. Clara says, 'I need a room for this, I need a room for that,' and then I build it. We're going to have to call it the Winchester Mansion pretty soon. Who's playin' that great music?"

We looked into the living room and there was Coco Delgado with her guitar and Moses T. Hyman on the fiddle. Their voices melded together like Peanut butter and jelly, like butter and toast. Kyle, my college age friend and employee sat Indian-style on the floor in front of Coco and T. H. with his girlfriend, Kelly. They were completely immersed in the old Christmas carols

Cajun-style, while Solow and Tansey raced around the room barely missing a tree named Bob. Bob looked like an over-barbered shrub smothered in bobbles and bangles, lights and tinsel.

Monica, Laurita, Trigger and the twins ran through the house and out the back door. Solow and Tansey followed. Deciding to help Robert keep an eye on the twins, I made my way through the crowd to the deck on the other side of the hot tub where Harley was working the barbecue with an old friend of mine, Steve, owner of the paint store in Watsonville where I usually bought my paint.

Just when I thought I'd seen everyone, Officers Lund and Sayer marched across the patio and stood in front of me with blank faces. Were they here to spoil the party? I stood up to say hello. Out of curiosity many of the partiers moved in behind the officers, including David.

"What are you doing here…?" I stammered, visualizing handcuffs and a stiff warning about poking into other people's business.

Officer Sayer stepped closer to me and shook my hand. When he smiled, I finally put a little energy into the handshake. Why was everyone whispering?

Many thoughts raced through my head, thankfully most of them would prove to be wrong.

"David told us about your party," Denise Lund said, "and we decided to come by and thank you for your help in solving Mary Milford's murder."

Wow, that was the nicest thing she'd ever said to me. I was stunned.

"You did a great job, Ms. Stuart," Sayer said, "but please don't try that risky stuff like hanging from a balcony again. Give us a call next time." He smiled.

It seemed like everyone had crowded onto the patio, but why were they being so quiet? Obviously, they were listening to the officers, but when Lund and Sayer left, everyone stayed. David walked up to me and handed me a small black box with a red ribbon tied around it. At first, I imagined a pretty pair of earrings.

David got down on one knee….

Oh no, it must be crunch time, I thought, *time to choose my path for the second half of my life*.

So many thoughts—so many decisions—so little time. I looked across the crowd of smiling friends and family and glommed onto Mom and Dad standing with Aunt Clara and Uncle Ben. I was staring at two couples—two good cases of real love that lasts through thick and thin, the kind of love I knew I would have with David. I checked my watch. It was 8:08, a strong "yes." But I didn't say *yes* or *no;* the kiss said everything.

The clapping, whistling, whooping and happy smiles of my friends and family lasted through another kiss and then some.

The Mary Christmas celebration had begun.

But one more surprise was about to be unveiled. Alicia held a wrapped Christmas present in her hands. She walked up to David and me wearing a little smile that grew wider as she handed David the present.

Thirty-five people stood watching, silent as plum pudding.

"David and Josephine," Alicia announced, "let me be the first to give the happy couple a Christmas present. Every time you see it, you will remember this day."

David pulled the wrapping paper away, exposing a framed picture. I recognized the frame as a 'Buzz' frame. But when I saw the painting, I was overjoyed. Alicia had bought the picture I'd painted of Fluffy at the Art Festival and now she made sure David would have it. He held the picture above his head and turned it right to left for everyone to see.

I looked around at all the happy faces and wished Mary could be with us. I felt a woosh of air across the back of my neck and looked over my shoulder to see if Mary was there, and then I checked my watch. It was 8:22 and the Christmas party had one more ghost—I mean, guest.

Epilogue

Needless to say, Marla continued to be instrumental in Laurita's upbringing. Once Juanita lost her freedom, things changed quickly for the better. Marla and Mel took Pedro to see a specialist. They were surprised and happy to learn that he had simply broken a hip bone that could be replaced. A few months later, after the hip-replacement operation, he donated his wheelchair to the Salvation Army and went to work for a contractor named Mel.

Mel's injuries from falling off Josephine's roof healed and he went back to work, winning a large contract with the city. Mel bought a town house and helped Pedro interconnect the four rooms in the garage to make a better home for Laurita and her dad.

Kirby was thrown in jail for lewd acts.

Claudia, Vick and Buzz combined their historical knowledge of Capitola and wrote a book called, *Fifty Shades of Capitola.*

Mom and Dad signed up for Jake's surfing class.

I went back to painting murals for a living because it was what I loved to do—no phone calls, no interruptions—just paint.

David continued to be the best-looking, nicest guy in town and he was promised to me. The thought gave me goose bumps, better known as "happy bumps." The only problem with our future marriage would be living with Solow and Fluffy in the same house. I couldn't imagine it.

THE END

ABOUT THE AUTHOR

Author Joyce Oroz takes her past experiences as a mural artist and tucks them neatly into her stories as needed. Real life for Oroz these days consists of adventures with the grandchildren, large gatherings with family and friends and the day-to-day reading, writing, painting, walking the dog and battling invading packs of gophers. She loves her husband, dog and California routine. Writing is the sweet topping on her busy life.

The Josephine Stuart Mystery Series by Joyce Oroz

Who Murdered Mary Christmas?
Scent of a $windle
Roller Rubout
Cuckoo Clock Caper
Beetles in the Boxcar
Shaking in Her Flip Flops
Read My Lipstick
Secure the Ranch

Proof

61674754R00135

Made in the USA
Charleston, SC
22 September 2016